Leaving Still Waters

a story about arriving together

Marcus Cary Hondro

Don't forget to read it! Thanks mum Hnd

1.

The sun is beginning to dip below the horizon as James and Lana Miller drive down the highway that runs alongside of Lake Still Waters. The gas tank is full, the roof rack on their mid-sized sedan is loaded and their spirits are cautiously high.

It is July but it is stormy and Lana, in the passenger seat, looks out the window at the trees on the side of the lake as they sway in the wind and rain.

"Too bad it was such a wet parade," she says.

"It certainly was."

"I guess we should have left after it was over."

James loves that his wife is a doting mother and despite the weather insisted on cooking their children supper and then decided they'd sit and eat with them. Setting up camp will be more of a challenge now but he's just happy they're on their way, that they are really doing it, just the two of them. No children, not this time.

"Well it was nice to have dinner before leaving," he says, smiling as he reaches his hand out to settle upon her knee. "It felt good for all of us to sit down together."

"Not that they stayed still long. God, Riley is constantly on the move and Keeley is forever moving her lips."

"She does like to talk."

A sudden bolt of lightning followed by a loud crack gets James thinking about the task ahead. "In this weather setting up that tent might be fun," he says.

"We should call them every day," Lana blurts out.

"No, no we said we'd trust they'd be okay, which they will," James says. "Besides, the campsite might not have a public landline; everyone has a mobile nowadays."

"Except us," Lana replies, pointedly.

"You wanna get one, go ahead. I still don't think we need them and last time we talked about it you didn't either."

"I know I didn't. And I remember you telling me how according to some study people check their phones two-hundred and fifty times a day. Crazy."

"I think it was two-hundred and fifty-*three* times a day, to be exact."

"Well we can make a pact to keep it down to one-hundred and fifty-three."

"Everything will be fine. They will be fine, okay?"

"Well I did tell Keeley and Riley we'd call."

"And I told Norman we only call *if* we could."

Seeking to change the subject, he tells his wife he hopes Norman will refer to the storm as a "summer squall" in the family newspaper, the Still Waters Current.

"I love the alliteration," he says. "Or it's a sort of alliteration."

"Summer squall? It's not alliteration at all," Lana tells him. "Besides, Norman's not big on alliteration and he'll just call it a storm."

"You're right. Anyhow, storm or squall, it should clear by morning and we'll have wonderfully warm weather for camping. How's that for alliteration?"

A green pick-up truck passes and speeds off. James was looking over to his wife and didn't pay it any attention, but Lana saw the truck. They know the driver and she wonders where he's going but the man is a subject she's reluctant to bring up.

Despite the wet weather the pick-up is going over the speed limit and quickly disappears. A mile further along, with no traffic in sight, the driver does a U-turn and pulls over to the shoulder of the highway. He turns off the ignition and, wobbly, climbs out; a near-empty bottle of whisky rolls off his seat, tumbles out the door and smashes to the ground.

"Damn," he mutters.

He reaches into the back of the pick-up to grip, of all things, a javelin. He lifts it out then looks down at the broken bottle. A ruined life, he thinks, smashed. He considers again where the blame lies and draws the same conclusion he's drawn for 20 years. It wasn't his fault. It wasn't his wife's or son's, that's for damn sure. As headlights approach from the direction he came he mutters "It had nothing to do with us" and raises the javelin.

Back in the sedan, Lana has told James about the green pick-up passing and they are talking about its driver.

"I worry about him," she says. "He's such a loner. Keeps every-thing bottled up. We shouldn't have brought him here. Riley doesn't like him, you know."

"Keeley does."

"Keeley likes him because she senses you want her to. But she doesn't like him much. There's little for anyone to like."

"That's not true," James sighs. "And they'll get around to figur-ing each another out."

"It's been almost a year."

"Maybe with us being away he'll start to take an interest in them."

"We should have told Norman who he is."

"We tell them when Jack is ready, like we agreed. Now promise nothing will get in the way of this vacation." Lana rolls her eyes. "Come on. Say it. You gotta say it."

"God, you're worse than Keeley." He smiles at her. "Oh alright," she says. "I, Lana Miller, promise nothing will get in the way of our trip together. Not the weather, not the children, not Jack, not my penchant for worry and not *your* penchant for worry. And especially not the past. Done. Was that okay?"

"Yes, thank you, that was fine."

Lana turns to James and smiles and in that moment something crashes through the front windshield and lands in between them. Broken glass flies onto the Millers as James jerks the wheel to the right, careening toward the edge of the road. Lana screams. They hit a road sign and keep going, hurtling through bushes before disappearing over an embankment. Splash!

The car lands in the lake.

On the other side of the road stands the driver of the pick-up. He takes a few steps toward the bushes the car disappeared into, stops and sinks to his knees. An anguished moan as he covers his face, blocking his view from what he has just done.

He's up and running in the dark and rain. Across the highway, into bushes, face being scraped as he fights to reach the embankment. He looks down into the lake.

Jack calls out: "James? Lana?"

Back on the highway there is a repetitious pinging as rain falls against a half-bent aluminum sign that reads: 'You Are Now Leaving Still Waters.'

2.

Still Waters, British Columbia is an hour east of Vancouver along the Trans-Canada highway. Founded in 1858 and incorporated 100 years later, the town is named after nearby Lake Still Waters, named because of its low hydraulic gradients which, except during a storm, make the lake's surface appear completely still.

It is a hot July morning, three days after Canada Day, and we are in a friendly neighbourhood outside the Miller family residence. Their home sits in a row of typical, middle-class homes but stands out for it is a Class 'A' double-wide BigRunner motor home. The yard is like others, a white picket fence, a lawn, a small shed and a Sunrise apple tree. Hockey sticks and a net are strewn upon the ground, blown over in a recent storm and yet to be picked up.

Here's this: a motor home is not normally permitted in residential areas of Still Waters but upon their arrival 20 years ago the Millers took advantage of a poorly constructed municipal by-law, an oversight long since corrected. Their home is 'grandfathered' and can continue to sit where it is providing it *stays* where it is. Should it be driven off the lot it could not return and nor could another motor home take its place.

Only the two Miller boys live in it now, their parents and sister having moved into an apartment in back of the newspaper they own and operate. There wasn't enough room for everyone at the apartment and besides, the motor home suits Norman and Riley just fine.

As owners of the well-respected local newspaper the Miller family has good standing in the community. Still, some neighbours find the motor home a giant eyesore. James and Lana have done their best to make it presentable, painting it a deep green with a handsome blue trim and hanging a row of flower boxes on the side, the bright blue hydrangeas nearly matching the color of the trim. The maintenance is kept up, though not so regularly nowadays, and the engine is turned over, though that, too, is no longer done on a regular basis. Of course it hasn't been driven since the day it arrived and the Millers cannot say if it is capable of moving one inch let alone out the yard and down the road.

They will soon find out.

James and Lana Miller bought a movable home out of fear they may one day need to make a quick escape. Twenty years ago a terrible event involving two family members lead to their fleeing Vancouver for Still Waters and they felt a mobile home would be a prudent choice in the event they were forced to flee again. They never told their children about running from their past, instead telling them the reason they left Vancouver was because they sought a small-town lifestyle and wanted to own a community newspaper.

There are other things they have not told their children, such as the fact that before moving to Still Waters they changed their surname and considered changing their given names (they likely would have had the internet been so prevalent back then). Neither did they tell them that after moving they stopped communicating with old friends and began life almost entirely anew.

They ran hard and fast from the past.

On this day in the present from inside the motor home comes the voice of the demanding Keeley Miller, 10 years-old and as fiery as a comet with a dimpled nose and a page-boy haircut. Heard along with Keeley is her 13-year-old brother, the ever-inquisitive Riley Miller, sporting a crew-cut in the summer because he feels he runs the bases faster without hair. Riley sits at a small table in the tiny kitchen area finishing toast with marmalade and reading a Science Digest. He is also quarrelling with his sister, hardly an unusual occurrence.

"It will take you five minutes," Keeley yells.

"Well I don't got five minutes," Riley yells back.

"You are so selfish! Yuck-head!"

Keeley is a few feet away behind a bedroom door, normally Riley's bedroom but now, temporarily, being used by Keeley, for she could not stay alone in the apartment at the newspaper office during their parent's absence. Just now she wants Riley to get her a muffin and juice from a nearby café but running errands for his little sister is not Riley's idea of fun. Besides, why doesn't Keeley simply walk the two blocks to Alf's Café and get her own muffin and juice? Still Waters is a safe community and she's gone there and back on her own many times.

Riley is right, Keeley has walked to that cafe many times and Still Waters is a safe community. But she will not go there today because yesterday morning she locked herself inside of her (again, technically Riley's) room and is refusing to come out.

Keeley often locks herself in her room when change occurs, even minor change, such as when her mother joined the local reading club or her older brother Norman stopped seeing a girlfriend she liked. This time it is over her parents. Since leaving three days ago James and Lana haven't called and Keeley, in possession of an active imagination, has decided something happened, something bad like "they were in an accident" or they were "kidnapped by someone mean."

She insists Norman go and find them and until he does the door to her (technically Riley's) room will remain locked from the inside.

Here's this: there's no pressing need for her to come out for she has everything she might need inside of that room. There's a portable toilet, an Enviromatic-FlushAway, recently installed because she refused to share a bathroom with her brothers. Her food is being passed to her via a slot in the middle of the door, originally a mail slot as the door was once the front door at the newspaper office. Only boredom could force Keeley out and given her love of books and music and being in the possession of a laptop, she is not likely to be bored.

In any case, Keeley Miller announcing she is not leaving her room until her parents return means that Keeley Miller is not leaving her room until her parents return. You'd have a better chance of getting your average teen to give up texting than you would of coaxing her out before she is ready.

"Norman!" Keeley calls out. "Norman, Riley is being selfish again!"

In the motor home's only other room, on the other side of where Riley sits and also feet from the table, a sleepy Norman Miller opens his eyes and frowns. He doesn't like his siblings to quarrel, especially if it's the first thing he hears upon waking. Rubbing sleep from his eyes, he sits up in his bed, inches from the cot Riley is using while their parents are away. Norman is six feet tall and has dark hair that makes it down to the top of his ears. His face, often described by young women as cute, usually has upon it an expression that suggests he is annoyed with the world, which he frequently is.

He reaches out and opens the door, takes but one step and he's in the kitchen.

Riley looks up. "Hey morning, Bro," he says.

"Good morning. You know it'd be nice to have just one morning without a fight."

"No problem," Riley tells him. "Only Keeley thinks I'm her personal servant."

"Some servant," Keeley calls out. "I'd die of starvation before you helped me."

"Don't get my hopes up!"

"Okay, enough." Norman points a finger at Riley. *Do not ever make a joke like that about your sister again. She is precious. Understand?"

Riley scoffs. "Precious? Norman, the Dweller in the Room is crazy. She's gone nutso in there."

"No, she hasn't. She's just worried. Come in here," he gestures to their bedroom. "Come on " Riley follows his big brother into the room. Norman closes the door. "You need to get along with her," Norman whispers. "We told Mom and Dad we'd take care of her while they were away and getting her whatever she needs is part of that. So please, go."

Riley also whispers. "You mean we told our Mom and Dad who are missing, that Mom and Dad?" (Riley, for once, agrees with his sister and is convinced something has happened to their parents).

"Riley, no. They just haven't called. That's not so unusual. Now what does she want this time?"

"She wants to shove a raspberry muffin and peach juice down her gullet but I got a life," he quietly pleads. "Me and Arjun and Geoff are going to catch herring at the creek before shooting hoops; besides, I got her stuff yesterday and it made me late for cliff diving."

Norman tells Riley he doesn't want him cliff diving and reminds him he might have to write a story for the next edition of the paper.

"But after that last stunt I'll be keeping a close eye on the content," Norman adds. "I'll be keeping an close eye on all your stories for a long while."

As he marches his little brother the few steps to the front door, Norman asks where he learnt the word 'gullet.' He likes Riley and Keeley improving their vocabulary and when Riley tells him he must have read it in a book, Norman tells him to keep reading.

"And go get your sister her raspberry muffin and peach juice. Right there and right back, thank you."

Keeley calls out, "And if they don't have the raspberry make it the lemon and cranberry and if they don't have the lemon and cranberry get the raisin. They always have the raisin."

"Yes, Mistress Keeley." The door opens and Riley is gone.

"Thank you, Norman," Keeley calls out.

"Do you think you could ask him nicely next time?" he says. "It might help."

"I could try. I guess. I'd rather not. Joking!"

Back in his room, Norman starts to dress for work. Most days he wears a rumpled brown suit, his personal dress code for a serious journalist, and that is what he puts on today, with his favorite blue paisley tie. His suits make him feel like a big-city reporter from a bygone era but he could conduct an interview in a lumberjack shirt and no one would care. He's been writing for the *Current* since he was 8 (a review of his spelling test) and everyone knows and likes him. He's had girlfriends but while at first they're happy to go out with a guy who writes stories in the local paper, before long his absorption with his work turns them away.

Truth is Norman would rather write than go to a movie or play sports or do pretty much anything. He is especially fond of new journalism and Still Waters is routinely treated to features and profiles written in a style rarely seen in a small-town paper. In-depth stories with titles like 'Fun and Laughing in Still Waters' or 'Mayor Alice Cormier has a flu.' The former, written at 15 and inspired by Hunter S. Thompson's 'Fear and Loathing in Las Vegas,' was about a group of kids, jacked up on sugar after a soda drinking contest, literally herding cats to a swimming hole for a bath. The latter, written last year, was about a day spent with Still Waters' grumpy Mayor Cormier and mimicked Gay Talese's famous 1966 Esquire piece, 'Frank Sinatra has a cold.'

Norman aims high – and succeeds.

Suit on and shoes tied, he stands, grabs his notebook and stuffs it into his back pocket. He wistfully looks over to a photo of James and Lana. This is not an easy time. In his parents absence he has extra responsibilities both at home and at the paper, plus he, too, is worried about the fact they did not arrive at their camp-site. He is almost certain they went somewhere more remote and, not having a mobile, couldn't call and tell him. His father often changes plans, and is good at talking his mother into going along with it, so he's not too worried but yeah, he's a little wor-ried. He pushes it from his mind.

Ten minutes later he is holding open the door-slot in Keeley's bedroom door with his left hand while his right holds a bowl of oatmeal. He does not mind Keeley having a muffin, Riley de-livered her one and rushed off, but he likes her to eat oatmeal.

"Come on, Keeley. Please. It's good *and* good for you."

"You make oatmeal too lumpy."

"I do not."

"Yes, you do." She pushes something through the slot, a small fire axe. "Here. Mister Smart-Apple Riley said all the knives were dirty so gave me the fire ax to butter and slice my muffin. He was trying to annoy me but it worked fine, so the joke is on him."

Norman takes it. "Great. An axe for a muffin. I'll speak to him." He wipes off the blade and puts it in the nearby storage cupboard and gets back to the subject of Keeley's breakfast.

"Listen, it's not much oatmeal and I stayed right by the stove and stirred it frequently. I swear it's not lumpy. Mine tastes great."

"Sorry Norman but we'll have to talk about something else. For example, did you know that Canada Day on Saturday was our sesquicentennial Canada Day? And that we spent nearly half-a-billion dollars on celebrations? I bet you didn't."

Norman gives up on Keeley and oatmeal and sits working on his own, rather lumpy, bowl of it. "No I didn't but I'm happy you're learning," he says. "Only don't spend too much time on the internet. And I expect sesquicentennial refers to our country's 150th birthday."

"Smart."

"Say," he says. "I got a great story for the paper. Mister Mahortoff grew a pumpkin the size of a smart car. He sent me a picture; biggest I've ever seen." He waits. Nothing. "Well, I find that interesting."

"Well I sure don't."

"He's gonna bring it down to the office today." Norman is not only trying to get Keeley to come out of the room, he loves seeing her byline in the paper. "You know you could come by, do the interview, write the story. You haven't written anything for awhile."

"Nice try but I'm not exactly fascinated by pumpkins. Most people aren't, in case you didn't know."

"I'll give you front page, right below the fold."

"I would not want front page below the fold. My friends would laugh at me for putting a pumpkin story on the front page. They're not newspaper illiterate, you know."

"Yes but I'll put the park zoning story above the fold and something soft below would be perfect. With your touch it'll be great."

"I don't have a touch, I'm ten. And besides, you do all these edit things to my stories anyhow."

"I do it for clarification and to help you learn." Frustrated, he gets to the problem at hand. "Listen, Keeley, if Mom and Dad were lost I promise I would go and find them. But they went on a camping trip and decided on somewhere more remote than the public site they booked. They'll be back in a few days."

"I don't believe you and I don't want the pumpkin story and I am staying right where I am. Period."

Norman sighs and empties Keeley's uneaten bowl of oatmeal into a small compost container. He uses his reflection in the toaster to straighten his tie.

"Norman?"

"Yes, I'm still here."

"You know that I love you, right? That you're the best brother, *ever*."

"And you know that I love you and you're the best sister, *ever*. And let's not forget about Riley."

"The question is: are you going to leave me? Because if you love me you wouldn't do that. Not ever."

"Well, I am not going to leave you, not ever."

"So you are never ever ever going to leave me? Is that right?"

"That is correct." He's hoping that's all she wants today.

"Good," Keeley tells her brother. "Except you have to say it like I did or it means you *are* going to leave me."

"Which I am not."

She wants him to say it. She always wants him to say and he always does what she wants. "I am never ever ever going to leave you," he says. He picks up his tattered briefcase. "Only right now I have to go to work. But as I have explained before that is not the same as leaving you." He moves to her door. "We talked about this and you agreed. I am simply going to work."

"I don't remember any such agreement."

"And Keeley, please don't press the button today; you're like the boy who cried wolf. You don't always need me or Riley to help you with something. If you have a problem maybe you could simply leave the room and walk down to the newspaper."

"You know that's not happening until you find them."

Norman sighs. "All right. Suit yourself. Just don't press the button all the time. I'll be back for lunch. I love you."

"Could you bring Paige back for lunch? I like her."

"We broke up two months ago; I told you that already."

"Well maybe you could get back together."

"She stopped answering my texts."

"You should have gone to that Snarky Puppy concert with her. You might keep a girlfriend if you did fun stuff like that instead of working all the time."

"Somebody has to work." He walks to the front door. "All right, I gotta go; I'll see you at lunch."

As Norman opens the door his briefcase spills open and much of its contents fall out onto the floor. Frustrated, he kneels and picks up papers and pens and stuffs them back in. He gets it shut but fails to notice his new bank card is still on the floor.

"Norman?" Sniffles from behind Keeley's door. "You're not leaving, are you?"

If he's to get to work, Norman knows he must stop engaging with her. He opens the front door. "Norman?" He steps outside, grits his teeth, and slowly closes the door behind him.

Silence.

Then: "Norman? NORRRMANNN!"

3.

The retired couple across the street from the Miller family are fond of saying there are but a finite number of summers in our lives and that we must relish each day of every one of them. Just now the two are in their front yard relishing this hot July day by engaging in their favorite activity: gardening. Margaret, slender, white, long gray hair and a yellow sun hat, is crouched and digging in the ground. Next to her, pulling out weeds, is Agnes, dark skinned, she's First Nations, with a round figure and reams of gray hair pinned up in a bun. They have a large garden in their backyard and are working on adding one in the front.

James and Lana Miller, it was Lana's idea, asked them to keep an eye on their children while they were away and Agnes and Margaret took the job to heart. On this morning they would like to speak with Norman about a story they read in the newspaper that has caused them to be concerned. Norman comes hustling out his gate and Agnes calls out a hello. He waves and smiles.

"We only read your latest paper this morning," Agnes says.

"Well I hope you enjoyed it."

"A certain story was a cause for alarm," Margaret says.

"The park zoning story? I'm gonna do a follow-up in the next edition and I'll list the options as they were presented to council. I covered the meeting last night."

"You know very well what we mean," Margaret says.

Agnes says, "The story you wrote about your parents, about

their being missing."

Margaret adds, "We'd like to help in any way we can."

Norman figured they might ask about this particular story, they aren't the only ones, since the latest edition came out he's fielded phone calls and had to explain what happened to people on the street and in shops.

"I can explain that," he tells them. "In point of fact Riley wrote that story and it's basically fiction. He and Keeley aren't used to them being away and they've both let their imagination run wild."

"Riley wrote it?" Margaret asks.

"Yeah. I should have known he was up to something when he volunteered to do layout; he hates lay-out. I told him to put the Canada Day parade story on the front but he buried it inside and put his story there instead."

"But your byline is on the story," Margaret says.

"He wanted to give it more impact. I didn't catch it until the template was at the printers. It also got picked up by the Telegraph in the city. Very unfortunate and we're getting calls of concern but really, they're fine."

Agnes says, "So you've heard from them have you?"

"No, but I didn't expect to. You know my parents, free spirits." Norman smiles. "Your garden is coming along. It looks great."

"We haven't planted anything yet," Agnes points out. "We're digging it up for the late season."

"Well, you've done a grand job of digging."

Margaret still isn't satisfied everything is okay with the children. "Norman, I do wonder, since your parents left Riley is forever coming and going. But not Keeley. We haven't seen Keeley even once. We hear her, however, wailing as she does."

"I call it caterwauling," Agnes chirps in.

"We hope she's not sick."

"Sick? No. She's a vocal kid. Learned behavior. Whenever she screamed my parents gave in to her," Norman really wants to get to work and to end this conversation. "She's just keeping to herself. Anyhow, I better get down to the paper. Enjoy your gardening."

He waves and is off.

Margaret nods her head at Agnes and kneels down and picks something up from behind a shrub. It is a video camera.

Moving out of their yard and down the street and, trying not to be noticed by him, Agnes and Margaret begin to follow Norman. Margaret turns on the camera and starts filming him. The two are indeed keeping a close eye on the Miller children.

Norman soon arrives at a cross street. Traffic is light. A car approaches and stops; Norman waves the car on but the driver of the car waves Norman on; Norman, however, like many of us, was taught not to cross even when the driver waves you on and so instead, once again, he waves the driver on; the driver replies in kind and the two are at a standstill.

"Here we go again," Agnes says.

Simultaneously the car and Norman move forward. They stop. Each again waves the other on. The driver takes her hands off the wheel and thrusts them out the window – she looks like she's doing the wave at a hockey arena, only permanently to the left – to indicate she has no intention of moving until he passes.

He begins to cross but a car coming the other way screeches to a halt. It's Meyrick Pahl, a local who's been through this. Norman retreats back into the first lane where that driver had begun moving forward but now brakes. Norman stands frozen in the middle of the road.

"Sorry," he calls to the drivers. "I just like to be sure."

Pahl puts his vehicle in park and gets out, indicating to the driver of the other car to do likewise. "It's quicker," he tells her. The woman exits her vehicle and Meyrick indicates with a sweeping arm gesture that Norman can cross. Norman crosses and the drivers get back into their vehicles and away they go.

As Norman enters a small wooden building with a sign on the window that reads *Still Waters Current*, Margaret unshoulders her camera.

"He was quicker today," she says.

4.

The Rainy Day Diner in downtown Vancouver is a classic retro diner with tubular steel-framed chairs, Naugahyde vinyl and laminated two-legged tables. Each table has a jukebox but Earl Porter, who does not care for rock music, or music at all, ignores his. A balding, big and beefy white guy, Earl sits at a window table over breakfast with his son, Benjie, 23, chubby and short at 5'6" with wavy dark hair and a gentle brown face. Benjie would love to play the jukebox – he's fond of love songs – but knows his father would never allow it.

Until the age of nine, Benjie was required to be deferential and his father, a devoutly religious man, lectured him daily about how they must "pierce the darkness" and prepare for the rapture. He was allowed no music or television and given only books acceptable to the religious congregation the family is a part of. If he transgressed the rules his father laid out, for example if he did not recite each of a multitude of prayers before bed, he would be locked in his closet until Earl remembered to open the door. Benjie spent entire nights in there.

When he was nine his father was sent to a federal prison for murder and remained there for thirteen years. His mother, Benilda, from the Philippines, loved her husband, and believed in his innocence, but did not like how restrictive he was with their son and after Earl was locked away she began giving Benjie more freedom. She also enrolled him in martial arts training to help him with self-esteem, for after all those years with his father he had little of that. To a degree it worked but upon Earl's release two years ago Benjie and his father went back to the same dynamic they had all those years before. Benjie, however, is trying to work toward a relationship that is not wholly dependant upon his being subservient. He has been at it for some time with limited success.

Benilda died of cancer six months before Earl's release but not before she made her son swear he would always respect and obey his father, such obedience to the dominant male of the family an important part of her upbringing. Benjie was devoted to his mother and wants to keep his promise and so engages in a balancing act, on the one hand doing as his father bids, on the other working to establish a degree of independence.

At the moment, Earl has a newspaper in one hand and a lit cigar in the other and is lecturing his son on the necessity of a healthy breakfast. When it comes to food, Earl has confused large with healthy, doubtless a big reason why he's so large. Benjie is busy reading the words of Freidrich Nietzsche, the 19th century German philosopher, and has eaten little. The owner of the diner, Lindsay Wade, walks up and glowers at Earl, who mutters under his breath as he stubs out his cigar on a saucer. Lindsay walks off as Earl scoops eggs and pancakes onto a fork and jams it into his mouth while continuing to talk.

"The amount of fuel in your car tells you how far you can go," Earl says. "Did any of those fancy books ever teach you that, son?"

Benjie is accustomed to his father's ambiguous declarations and has been responding with ambiguity of his own, which he reasons is a step in the direction of becoming less subservient. He now tells Earl they didn't have cars when the authour of the book he is reading was alive. Wonderfully ambiguous and off the point yet more or less true as Nietzsche died in 1900 when automobiles were in their infancy.

"What I'm trying to teach you is everything is connected," Earl says. "Your shoelaces, your shoes; your hair, your comb; your pancakes, your body. Family. Country. Money. God. Reverend Broom would tell you one and the same thing."

"Sure, Dad, I know he would."

Now during their breakfast together if either Earl or Benjie were to turn their head and look out the diner's window and across the street they would see a four-storey brick and mortar apartment building. The building was built in 1953 and predates The Rainy Day Diner by five years. In that building 21-year-old Casey Collier is staring out of her third-floor window. Casey, tall, ethnically Chinese with black hair to her shoulders, is not looking into the diner at the moment, though she could and on occasion does, no Casey is watching the phone booth that sits on the sidewalk in front of the diner. She is engaged in a task she hopes will lead to a new profession.

Adopted from Guangdong province in China at 8 months, Casey grew up suspicious of her place in her Canadian family and her place in the world around her. She is forever planning her next move. A recent next move was to enroll in a private detective course but while Casey is good at beginning things, she's not so good at finishing them. Unable to commit to the dull routine of a classroom, she dropped out after three months. But she still hungers to be a detective.

All she lacks is a case.

A neighbour from down the hall, Philip Briggs is visiting Casey at the moment. They once fooled around until Casey decided that Philip, four years older, wasn't her type. He's British and while she rather liked his accent she soon realized he was a guy who, before long, would look like one of those white stocky English dart players on the sports channel: thick bodied and entirely focused on something she is not the slightest bit interested in. Yet here he is back again, sitting on a stool with a hand reaching up to gently rub her back.

"Stop with the touching, Philip. We're through that stage."

"Really? What stage are we at now then?"

"Over here we call it 'just friends'."

"Oh yes, of course," he says, then hiccups. "We have that stage in England as well. It's bloody boring."

Casey ignores him and his hiccuping (when he drinks, which he often does, Philip hiccups) and focuses on the cumbersome electronic device sitting by her window. She leans over and turns up the volume. It's old but it was cheap and it is for bugging, for picking up, from a distance, telephone conversations. Her target just now is the phone booth in front of the diner and she is hoping to overhear a conversation that will lead to her first detective case.

Is that a good plan? A moral plan? She knows it is neither but reasons that even if she does not find a case she will get practice in snooping, which detectives must often do. As for the morality of it, Casey is trying to ignore that, telling herself that anything she hears which does not lead to a case she will never repeat and that should something lead to a case the good she will do will be reason enough for her ethical breach. Yes, she's justifying, and yes, she knows it.

But on she goes.

As Philip laughs about how "nobody uses a bleeding phone booth anymore" there's a click and a whirring sound as the device turns itself on. Casey triumphantly smiles and looks out the window to see a woman in the booth holding the phone's receiver.

"I am working," Casey tells Philip. "So keep quiet. Oh, and phone booths are not extinct; there are still dozens in this city alone; I did my research."

Through the headphones she listens to the unsuspecting woman's conversation and makes a sour face. Boring. The woman is telling a friend her iPhone won't charge and asks who will be at Deb's and at what time she should arrive. No case there.

Meanwhile, Philip's arm slowly finds its way up to Casey's shoulder, again. Frustrated by yet another dull conversation – she's been at this for the better part of three days – Casey yanks off her headphones and shoves the Brit off of his stool. He thumps to the floor.

"I told you, I'm working."

"In a manner of speaking so was I."

"No, you weren't. You were being annoying. Yet again. I could have you charged."

"God, if you keep rejecting me like this you'll give me a bloody complex."

"Good; at least then something about you won't be simple."

Right about now most men she's had in her life skulk off. But not Philip, who promises her he will work at getting used to being just friends and offers to make her "a nice cuppa tea." God, the British and their tea! And pluck! Casey admits she finds him amusing and reasons that underneath his lack of self-control and neediness lurks a decent human. She accepts the offer of tea.

As for Philip, he made his appearance in Canada less than a year ago, after having been rejected by a local bar maid in his home city of Sunderland. While he took his broken heart and left England, he did so without leaving his employment as an I.T. guy, or as he calls himself, "a surfer nerd on a keyboard." The renewable energy company he worked for told him he could continue in their employ from his new country. In Sunderland he began work at 9 a.m. Greenwich Mean Time and translated to the west coast of Canada that has him commuting from his bedroom all the way to his living-room and working from 1 a.m. until 9 a.m. Pacific Standard Time, Monday to Friday. This has created a confusing lifestyle and made his acclimation into Canadian life all the more difficult, which made him rely heavily on his first Canadian friend, one Casey Collier. He soon fell in love with her and now finds himself in the same situation in his new country as he had been in his old one: pining for a woman who has spurned him.

You can run, as they say, but you cannot hide.

Through her headphones, Casey hears the woman in the phone booth hang up. She looks out the window to see a 30-something woman, in plaid shorts and a grey hoody, come out from the phone booth and trudge off. "God, she even looks boring," Casey mutters.

Casey reminds herself to be patient. If you listen, she thinks, they will talk. Staring into the diner's window, she looks to see if she can spot the owner, Lindsay. She squints...is that Lindsay standing by the window table talking to two men? It is but now she moves on.

Philip asks, "Where are the Viva Puff cookies you keep round here?"

"I hid them from you. I'll get them." Up Casey gets.

Back in the diner, Earl is telling his son about the glorious days the future holds for their religious congregation once they relocate. Benjie can't see any glory and feels it a good time to ask about the direction the congregation is taking.

"But why did Reverend Broom pick Guyana?" he asks. That question has weighed upon his mind since his father told him about the move to South America. "I know the ministry needs to be built up again. But why can't we stay here?"

"The Canadian government is doing everything it can to shut us down and the U.S. doesn't want us, either," Earl says. "Guyana has a deeply religious base and there is an unused compound that suits our needs. It was built by another sect that broke off from the Seventh Day Adventist church and abandoned years ago."

"Yeah, Dad, I know, Jerry told me. But that was the sect run by the Reverend Jim Jones. And that compound has been empty for decades because of the Jonestown Massacre. Where over 900 people died."

"Yes, yes, that's the one."

"Who would want to work in God's name there?"

"True religious adherents will prepare for the rapture wherever like-minded disciples gather," Earl tells his son. "And remember: Mister Jones lost his way. Reverend Broom won't make the same mistake. We will be raptured and He will come again. Now finish eating."

"What about what's left of his ministry here?"

"Some will come now, others will follow later. There'll be a website to attract new adherents from around the world. Our ministry is going international."

Benjie says, "I guess a well-designed website would attract people. Tell them to make sure they put Reverend Broom's speeches up. He really is a good speaker."

"He's an orator, Benjie, and a brilliant one. He once had a TV audience of two million. Soon he'll have more. Now finish your nourishment."

"Yeah, but you know the thing is that going to a place where such a terrible thing happened is, well, bad karma, don't you think? Dad?"

Earl isn't listening any more, he's transfixed by something in the newspaper; a story has caught his attention and he's quickly reading through it.

"Wait. I know these faces," Earl says, pointing at the paper. "As

Jesus is my savior I swear it's them. Benjie, give me your phone."

"You said I look at it too much so I left it in the car."

Clutching the paper, Earl leaps up, knocking over his coffee. Shouting at Benjie to get the bill, he rushes to the cash register and asks to use the phone. The cashier says it is for staff only and tells him there's still a phone booth on the street right outside the diner.

Earl barrels outside and into the booth, drops in coins and starts to dial. Across the street inside of Casey's apartment her device whirs loudly and kicks into gear. Passing the Viva Puff cookies to Philip, she picks up her headphones and looks out the window. She hears ringing and sees a large man in the confined space of the booth, the receiver in his left hand, his right hand impatiently tapping on the glass.

Click – his call is answered.

In the phone booth, Earl is talking into the reciever. "It's me," he says. "I got something big. A story in today's paper about a couple missing from a town called Still Waters. Last name Miller but they don't fool me."

Sitting in her apartment with her headphones on, Casey likes what she's hearing and is hopeful this could be the case she so badly wants.

"First names are James and Lana," Earl is saying. "Now try James and Lana only with a last name that begins with an h....yeah, I'm sure it's them. There's a photo, they're older but it's them. There's something else: the story is written by a guy named Norman Miller. Wasn't their kid named Norman?"

Out from the restaurant comes Benjie, reading Nietzsche as he walks. He glances up, sees his father in the phone booth, stops, stands, goes back to reading.

"Yeah, sure," Earl is saying into the phone. "You bet he does."

Then: "We're on our way." Earl hangs up, bursts out of the booth and rushes to his son. "Enough of that," he says. "We have been summonsed." He grabs Benjie's book and throws it into a garbage before steaming off down the street. Benjie retrieves his book and scrambles after his father.

In the building on the other side of the street up on the third floor, Casey pushes buttons on her outdated machine, rewinds the tape and cranks up the volume.

"Aren't you the whirling dervish?" Philip says.

"Quiet!" She hits the play button.

"...only with a last name that begins with an h ."

"You mean you think that...?" a second voice is heard saying.

"Yeah, I'm sure it's them. There's a photo, they're older but it's them. There's something else: the story is written by a guy named Norman Miller. Wasn't their kid named Norman?"

"The Lord works in mysterious ways," the second voice says.

"Yeah, sure," Earl says. "You bet he does."

"Get over here. Now. You're going on a mission."

"We're on our way."

Click. Casey hits the stop button.

"Is this legal?" Philip asks.

"That is not your concern," Casey tells him. She rushes to the computer and types in 'James Lana H' but finds nothing connected to the conversation she overheard. She writes James and Lana Miller and gets the story from the Telegraph the man in the booth must have been referring to. She sends it to her printer.

Philip says, "Why exactly are you doing this?"

"I'm being resourceful," she says. "Creating my own work opportunities. It's the Canadian way." She grabs the story off the printer. "May I borrow your car?"

"Sorry, it's in the shop."

"No problem, I'll take a bus." Casey grabs her coat. "Oh, if you have any time on your hands, be nice if you did the dishes. And don't forget to lock up. Bye."

She's out the door.

5.

The Reverend Vernon Broom sits behind his desk in his ostentatiously decorated home in a pricey Vancouver neighbourhood. The self-titled Reverend, 70, is tall and thin with a full head of gray hair he combs straight back. He has a bulbous nose and a lean, stern-looking face. Just now it is very stern-looking.

The Reverend is deep in thought.

Outside the window that is behind his desk the mountains and ocean are in full view. A beaming sun sits in a cloudless blue sky and lawns are chock full of crocuses, rhododendrons and other bright flowers. There are bees and birds and the Monarch butterfly has made a return. It is a beautiful day on the west coast of Canada but Reverend Broom takes no notice.

Along with furniture, the (again, self-titled) Reverend's home is decorated with religious paintings and icons, but none of it, not the furniture, the paintings, nothing, will be here by day's end. At the government's behest movers are taking everything to a storage facility where it shall remain until it is itemized and auctioned off. That 'everything' will include the very desk and chair the Reverend Broom is now seated upon.

Casually carrying a statue of the Virgin Mary in one hand and a copy of da Vinci's Last Supper in the other, a mover strolls by the open office door. Reverend Broom winces but there's nothing to be done about it. He looks down at the open bible that sits upon his desk; he has been reading and re-reading a passage in the Book of Deuteronomy. He suddenly looks up.

"Jerry!" he yells. "Get in here. Quickly."

Moments later, a flustered Jerry Broom, an evil-looking, thuggish man of 26, enters and takes up a meek position in front of his father's desk, hands folded in front. Blood shows through a bandage over the fingers of his left hand. In his right hand he holds a piece of paper.

"What is that you have?"

"A notice," Jerry says. "I found it on the garage door; there's another one on the front door. A mover told me a woman from the sheriff's office posted them." He drops the notice on his father's desk.

Disdainfully, the Reverend picks it up and reads: "*This home is being seized for non-payment of taxes. All goods forfeited* etcetera, *by order of Municipal Judge Raveer Doshi of the city of Vancouver.* Blah blah blasphemy." He crumbles the notice and tosses it on the floor.

"Don't give this treachery any further thought," he tells his son. "Something far more important has come up. We have an old score to settle. You're taking a trip."

"But shouldn't I do something about all these movers, Father? They're taking everything."

"We have no time to dwell upon that which we cannot change."

"So you don't want me to hit them?"

"I do not. Remember this: the Lord moves in mysterious ways."

"So the Lord doesn't want me to hit them?"

"That is correct. He only sets you in motion when He sees fit. Here: in chapter 35 verse 32 in the Book of Deuteronomy the Lord speaks of revenge thusly," Reverend Broom looks to the Bible and reads from the page he'd been staring at: "*It is mine to avenge. I will repay. In due time their foot will slip; their day of disaster is near and their doom rushes upon them.*"

Reverend Broom closes the bible and slowly nods his head. "Their day of disaster will soon be upon them."

His son starts nodding his head, and with vigour. "Yeah, sure," Jerry says enthusiastically. "That sounds, you know, that sounds good. So what do I do?"

"Earl called with news concerning the man I hold responsible for what is taking place here today. The original sinner."

"You mean the reporter who wrote those stories?"

"That is correct. That we should hear about this man after all these years on the very day the downfall of our ministry in this city is being completed, the treacherous downfall which his actions set in motion, I believe to be a command from God."

Jerry does a fist pump. "Yes!" he says.

His father looks on disapprovingly; Jerry straightens up. "Son, this will be an explosive undertaking and I need you at your best. You are going to a town called Still Waters to locate the residence of James and Lana Miller. I have lost my home and the Millers must lose theirs but for now I simply want you to find it, to see it with your eyes, and report back to me."

"Find out where James and Lana Miller live. Look at their home then report back to you. Got it."

Reverend Broom looks to his son's hand. "Now what happened? The dog bite you again?" Jerry nods. "We shall have to leave her here for now and pick her up later. She'll survive. Go and ready for your departure."

As Jerry leaves, two movers step into the room; Jerry scowls at them but moves on. "What is it?" the Reverend bellows at the movers.

"The desk," a mover says. "Sorry."

Reverend Broom stands, pushing his chair aside. After so many years this is it. He takes a last look at his office, now his former office, and, head high, for the final time, he walks out the door. Does it cause sadness? Not so much, not now it doesn't. For Earl's timely news has given him a renewed sense of purpose. It has given to him a goal, the kind of goal the Reverend Vernon Broom (self-titled) takes a great joy in achieving.

It is the goal of revenge.

6.

After twenty years of ignoring them, Jack Smith made an agreement with his brother and sister-in-law: in exchange for his abstinence from alcohol he would be hired as a reporter; as part of the agreement he insisted his identity be kept from James and Lana's children – like his brother, he changed his surname years before – until he was ready to return to the family

For one entire year he kept his promise but he has begun to drink again. It was all becoming so tiresome for Jack, writing stories about people and events he could not bring himself to care for.

And there was still that deep wound from long ago.

At the moment, he is in the cramped washroom of the Still Waters Current, perched upon the throne, lid down, taking a swig from a shot-glass; a bottle of Canadian Club whisky sits on the counter. The swig felt good. He pours another. That goes down well, too. One more. Done, for now, Jack washes out the glass and stuffs it behind a drainpipe underneath the sink, sliding the bottle in beside it. He checks the scrape on his face – he told Norman a cat scratched him – and walks out the door.

The office is a large space, four desks and a front counter where the public drops off ads and letters or voices complaints. The paper runs a small banner on the editorial page that reads 'If you read something you like in these pages tell your neighbour, if you read something you don't like – tell us!' The good people of Still Waters follow that dictum and it is not uncommon for locals to drop by and offer up opinions and complaints.

Norman is on the phone. "I am gonna run the story in our next edition, Mister Mahortoff, and thanks for placing an ad," he says. "Well sir it's a heck of a pumpkin. Biggest and best I've seen. Bye for now." He hangs up and tells Jack they're going to hit 16 pages again.

"Your father will be happy," Jack says.

"Now we just need more stories to put around all these ads I'm selling."

"No surprises from Riley this week I hope?"

"That's the last time he lays out the paper without my signing off on the end result. I think the phone calls expressing concern have finally stopped."

"He's an amusing kid, your brother. Reminds me of someone I grew up with."

"So you've said before."

"Bold guy, this guy that I knew. Undaunted by circumstances, you might say. Hey, if we're short this edition you can always profile a kid or a dog," Jack tells him. "Or interview a poor family and make everybody feel sorry for them. That kind of thing goes over big in a town like this."

Norman loves his community and feels part of his job is writing about children and animals and he takes pride in running stories that help families in need so Jack's suggestions sound like cynicism to him. He is not sure why his parents brought Jack on. The man is a good enough reporter but they were doing well before he showed up and Jack clearly doesn't like the work. He hasn't made friends in Still Waters and complains about the town and its people. Norman would like to get to know him better and thought he might get that chance with his parents away.

Not so far.

"Think I'll take a break," Norman says. "Wanna grab a coffee at Alf's?"

"No. Think I'm done for the day," Jack stands. "See you tomorrow." Jack grabs his coat from the back of his chair and is out the door.

Norman figures it's just as well, he has lots to do, like writing up a council story, a pumpkin story and laying out copy. Settling back in his chair, he can't help but think there's something about Jack his parents haven't told him but he has no idea what it might be.

He resumes hitting the keyboard.

7.

On the bus ride to Still Waters Casey read the story on the missing couple four times and with each read she became more convinced she'd found her first case. And a good one at that. Being young and optimistic she figured pretty much all she had to do was find the Miller family and tell them they were in danger and she was there to help. Presto case!

She stands outside the bus depot and is having a look about the town. It has the appearance of a nice community and people who pass by her offer up cheerful hellos. She notices signs on shops have an artistic flair, the painted lettering of the 'Alf's Cafe' sign has been done by someone with an interest in calligraphy and 'Big Boomer's Hardware' has drawings of colorful tools dancing around the letters. Her first impression of Still Waters is a good one and she wonders how comfortable she might feel in a small town like this.

She asks a passing kid where the office of the Still Waters Current is and if it's owned by the Miller family. The boy tells her the paper is a block to the left and says he goes to school with Riley Miller and the Millers have owned the newspaper "since before I was even born." Asking where they live, he points her in the opposite direction of the newspaper.

"Down that way one block, then you make a left," the boy says. "You won't miss it because it's the only motor home in the whole town."

Minutes later she is knocking on the motor home's door. No answer. She finds the door unlocked, opens it and peeks in. Quiet, no one in the cramped living area. It is messy, with books and magazines strewn about, dishes undone, clothes tossed willy-nilly; there's clearly not enough space.

Boldly, Casey steps in, avoiding a pair of socks and a pack of hockey cards that sit upon the floor. A bank card lays near the socks and she picks it up. It reads: 'Norman Miller.' She places the card on the table.

"Anyone home?" she calls. "Is Norman Miller home?"

"Hey? Who's there?" It's a girl's voice.

"Hi. Your door was unlocked. I've actually come to maybe help out. My name is Casey Collier and I'm looking for Norman Miller."

"My Mom and Dad taught me not to speak to strangers," Keeley says. "Or like not unless they're the police or something. Are you the police or something?"

"No. I just wanted to talk to Norman Miller. I'm looking to be of service. I don't bite."

Keeley finds a visitor exciting but she's not certain she should be talking to her while at home on her own. "You sound nice, I guess, and I like the name Casey for a girl," Keeley says. "But you can never be sure about people in the modern world."

"Are you Norman's sister?"

"Maybe I am," she's not ready to say too much. "Why do you want to talk to him?"

"I wanted to ask about your parents."

"You do?" Now here's a subject Keeley will talk about; she's hopeful for good news. "Do you know where they are, by any chance?"

"No, sorry," Casey says. "Why? Are they missing?"

"They disappeared and Norman won't go and look for them," Keeley tells her. "So if you do see him please tell him to hurry up and find them."

"Uhm, okay."

"The more people that tell him the more he might do it; so far it's only me and Riley. He works at the newspaper, in case you didn't know. If he's not there he's doing an interview, which can take ages because he walks or rides his bike everywhere. And I mean *everywhere*."

"That sounds healthy."

"No, that sounds annoying, especially if you have to go with him."

"I gather you are behind this door with the slot."

"Correct. And I'm not coming out."

"Okay." Casey pulls out a business card. "Look, I'll try him at his office but in case he comes home I'm sliding my card under your door. Tell him I was here."

"And you'll tell him to find our parents, right?"

"You got a deal."

"My name is Keeley Miller, by the way."

"Nice to meet you, Keeley Miller. Or nice to almost meet you. Okay. Bye."

"Bye."

As she goes out the front door, Casey looks back. She likes Keeley, vulnerable yet feisty. She gets a feeling as if she's somehow abandoning her but it makes no sense and she dismisses it.

Stepping outside, she sees a black Cadillac across the road; her detective radar should be up but she is, after all, new to this and she pays the car little attention. She turns toward the newspaper and walks off.

Inside the Cadillac, Jerry Broom sits in the driver's seat, Earl Porter in the passenger seat and Benjie is directly behind his father in the back. It was easy locating the place, Jerry told the first person they pulled up alongside they were cousins of the Millers and was given directions to the motor home. All three watch Casey come out of the yard and move down the street.

"I wonder who she is?" Jerry says.

"She has to be somebody," Earl replies.

"No kidding." Jerry watches Casey disappear around a corner. "I got an idea; something maybe we can do right now. I think my Dad's gonna like this. Yeah. A lot."

"But he just wanted us to get the address, to have a look around and drive right back."

"Oh but he'll love this. Especially on the day we lost our home and everything in it. Come on, me and you, Earl." He turns to Benjie. "You stay put right here; only don't look like you're doing anything."

"That'll be easy because I won't be doing anything."

"Nobody likes a smart-ass, Benjie," Earl tells his son. "Be a team player."

"Sorry, Dad."

Once out of the car Jerry and Earl check to make sure their guns are jammed snugly into the back of their pants. All systems are go and when Earl comes around the car and stands beside Jerry, Jerry nods at him and the two trudge purposely across the road.

In the motor home, Keeley comes out of her room and peeks out the front window hoping to catch a glimpse of Casey. Instead she sees two "horribly mean looking men" – the words she uses in her mind – in suits; one is overweight and old, the other fit and young. The men step through the gate of the motor home and Keeley flees back into her room.

Arriving at the front door the men take a look about to make sure no one watches and pull out their guns.

They don't bother to knock.

8.

Children are notoriously restless and by his nature Riley is notoriously more restless than your average restless child. James and Lana can scarcely believe they wound up with a child so willing to career into any situation. Norman did not turn out that way and with Riley being so adventurous they worked doubly hard to instill caution in Keeley, their youngest.

They chalked Riley's nature up to Second Child Syndrome and did their best to convince him to express himself in ways that did not involve perpetual motion and risk-taking. That seemed to serve as a gauntlet to Riley and as a toddler he was forever on the move and getting into things. He was often amusing and there's a series of photos of the three-year-old Riley, taken over a ten minute span, in which he's dressed as a baseball player, a fireman, a policeman, a Ninja soldier, Swiper from Max and Ruby and a turnip.

As Earl and Jerry walk uninvited into the motor home, Riley is restlessly moving about the office of the Still Waters Current. Norman, by his nature someone who thrives upon structure, is trying to divert his brother's attention to work. While he writes a zoning story, he asks Riley to write up the story about the pumpkin. Riley says there are more important things to do, like finding their parents.

"If they decided on a more remote campsite they would have found a way to tell us." Riley insists. Bottom line: he's not writing about a pumpkin.

While Norman works, Riley keeps moving. As he wanders, he

complains about their parent's no mobile phone rule and teases Norman for being the only adult in Canada who listens to his father when he tells him he doesn't need a phone.

"It's even more weird when you add in the fact that you're a reporter," he tells his brother.

"Riley, I have a land line and that's all I need," Norman says. "Humans went thousands of years without phones of any kind. Could you please stop walking around? You're making me dizzy."

Riley jumps up to a seated position on a corner of his father's desk. "If they had a mobile they could text us and tell us where they're being held hostage."

"I expect the first rule in kidnapping operational guides is *take away mobile devices*. Now enough about that. I have notes on Mister Mahortoff's pumpkin. It'll take you 30 minutes tops to write the story."

"I am going to be a great novelist one day and I don't want the press dredging up a story about a large, orange vegetable. Besides, a story on a giant pumpkin in a community paper is a giant cliché."

"Then be quiet so I can write it. Eat something. By the way: is a pumpkin really a vegetable?"

"What else would it be?"

"Yeah, I guess. It is huge. I have a photo. Massive. Size of those early space capsules. Those rounds things from the 60s. It's a one in a million pumpkin."

"Nice try, but I'm gonna go and hit golf balls."

As Riley moves toward the door it opens and Casey enters. She smiles at Riley, who decides he's gonna stay put. New people are fun and he's curious about her.

Looking up, Norman's first thought is that an attractive woman is standing at the front counter. She's dressed simply, black yoga pants and a white t-shirt, he likes that. But while his first thought was that she's attractive, his second is that it doesn't matter how good looking she is - he has work to do.

For Casey's part, she likes the guy at the desk. About her age. Longish hair. Cute face but he looks unhappy somehow. Annoyed perhaps. Maybe he's just busy. She figures she better play it cool, not be too pushy, but definitely let him know she's a professional.

She asks if he is Norman Miller.

"I am. But I'm afraid I have a deadline and we're closed," he tells her. "If you have an ad there's a form on the counter. It's too late to make the next edition though."

"I don't have an ad," she says.

"Okay. A complaint?"

"No complaint."

"Oh. Well if it's a story come back tomorrow."

"I don't have a story, either. My name is Casey Collier and I'm a private detective; from Vancouver."

"Cool," Riley says, hopping up and sitting on the counter next to where Casey stands, facing her. "Like murder cases and stuff?"

"Private detectives deal with all manner of crimes. Murder, robbery, assaults. We also get fraudulent insurance claims and standard marital infidelity cases. I do whatever pays the bills."

She fails to mention that those are the kind of cases she *might* get. In actuality, she hasn't had any cases.

Riley says, "So have you like taken pictures of guys, you know, like cheating? I mean in bed, with a woman? You know – like having sex with them?"

"Riley, did you have to ask that?"

"I'm curious."

"Private investigators handle those cases and I have a phone with a sophisticated camera and should that situation present itself I do my job, yes. It's part of being a detective. Like a private one, which is what I am."

Norman says, "You mentioned that."

Riley leans over to peek behind her back. "Do you carry a gun?"

"Riley, come on. Move away from her. It's obvious she doesn't have a gun." Riley slides about two inches over.

"I don't, no, but I do have a licence to carry," Casey is flat-out lying now. She put in an *application* for a licence to carry a gun but hasn't followed up because she never got her detective licence. "So I could, if I wanted. And I've been to a gun range." Another lie, it was a part of the course but she dropped out before they went.

"Oh yeah, cool," Riley is impressed.

"The thing is, if you say the right things, you really shouldn't need a gun," she tells the kid. "Uniform police in England don't carry them." She realizes she sounds defensive and shuts up.

Norman says, "Well if you had one you'd have to leave. I do not like guns."

"Norman thinks football is too violent and only barely likes hockey."

"That's not exactly relevant, thank-you, Riley. Now, Ms. Collier -

"Call me Casey."

"...as I've noted, I have a deadline so if you could tell me why you're here that would be helpful."

"I came to ask about a story of yours."

"This is a community newspaper; most weeks I write upwards of twelve stories."

"The one in the city paper about a missing couple."

"Sorry to disappoint you but the missing couple are my parents and in point of fact they are not missing."

Riley pipes in. "They haven't called. They never made it to their campsite. That's the definition of missing."

Casey walks over to stand at the side of Norman's desk. "I know this must be hard for you and we've just met. But anything you say to me is confidential. As I said, I'm a professional, a private detective."

"You did say that, yes."

"And I came here to help you."

"That's nice. In a weird sort of way. Only there's nothing to talk about. I expect while driving to the public campsite our parents made a decision to go somewhere else. These things happen."

Casey is convinced Norman is keeping something from her. "I was at your motor home; your sister made me promise I would tell you to find your parents. So like your brother, she's worried about them, too. Why?"

"First of all, Keeley gets people to make promises a lot. It's her thing, especially if she's in a worry phase, like she is now. She neglects to employ logic, however, or include facts. Like the fact that our parents are prone to changing their minds and don't carry a phone."

"Wow. No phone. Serious?"

"Serious. My father thinks they're addictive and unnecessary. He won't allow any of us to have one. You could say that he's a modern-day luddite."

Riley says, "No way. Luddites hated all technology and wanted everything to stay the same. We studied them in labour class. The word comes from a 19th century anti-industrial uprising in England. But dad doesn't hate all technology. Case in point: there are three computers and a printer in this office."

Casey says, "Kid's pretty smart."

"If backtalk is a sign of intelligence, he's brilliant. Now, as I keep saying: I have work to do."

Riley jumps in again, "Norman is afraid to admit they're missing because if he did then he'd have do something about it. He's aggressively passive."

"See what I mean about backtalk?"

On a desk next to Norman's a red light starts flashing; He presses it and it stops.

"That will be Keeley looking for her supper," Norman says. "She's not only given to worry, she's demanding."

"The flashing light is a signal from her?" Casey asks.

"She asked for a phone to reach us but instead our father had Richard, our maintenance guy, install an alarm in her room that sends a signal to that light."

"Which she uses all the time," Riley says.

"Riley, go and get your sister a sandwich and ask Alf to put it on my tab." Riley makes a face but hops down from the counter.

The light starts flashing again, Norman presses it again and it shuts off. It flashes again.

"She likes pressing it," Casey says.

"She wants me to come home." Norman presses the button and the flashing stops. It starts again. He presses the button and it stops and then starts again. "Riley, tell her I have two more stories." He presses the button again; it stops flashing. They are all staring intently at it, giving it their full attention.

It stays off.

"Finally. Okay. Go. Make it a lettuce and tomato on Italian with cheddar."

"But I was gonna hit balls into Bluewater," Riley grumbles, opening the door.

"I don't want you hitting balls into the park anyhow. Now get moving."

On his way out he warns Casey that Norman will try to get her to write a story. "But he only gives out the boring ones," he says. The door closes behind him.

Norman resumes typing.

Casey considers how to convince him to listen to her. She moves closer to his desk and plunges in. "I must say I am curious about something. It has me…stumped."

Norman stops writing and sighs.

"Why would you write a story about your parents being missing if you don't think they're missing?"

He goes back to writing. "I didn't write the story."

"It has your name on it."

Norman sighs, stops writing. "Riley wrote it. He knew it would get more attention with my byline. An editor from the city, Frank Lieske, picked it up for the Telegraph. He thought he was being helpful."

Attractive or not, Norman doesn't like a stranger asking questions. "Why are you here again and who exactly are you?"

"I told you, I have information pursuant to your case."

"And I told you: there is no case."

"I didn't want to say this in front of your brother but certain people are coming here to harm your family. I would call that a case."

"Where did you hear this and who are you again?"

These are tricky questions for the newly minted detective and she recalls one of the instructors of the course, the course she never completed, droning on about how detectives shouldn't reveal their sources. And should she tell him more about herself? That she is determined to finish something in her life and this case might be a perfect something to finish? Tell him she got her information by eavesdropping on a phone booth?

Nah.

"I am bound by professional ethics and can't reveal my sources," she says. "Sorry, but that's the way it is."

None of what she says makes sense to Norman and he considers that she might be mentally unwell. Though she looks young to be a real detective she appears normal – he again thinks of how attractive she is – but when it comes to mental health, appearances can be deceiving. He decides to exercise even more caution than he's already been exercising, exercising caution being something that he, and his family, save Riley, have historically been rather good at.

The bottom line for Norman is that it seems preposterous anyone would want to harm his family. While he does have a longstanding relationship with fear he simply cannnot believe they have enemies. It is far easier for him to believe that Casey Collier is mistaken and perhaps more than a little bit loopy.

"Look," he says. "They went somewhere more remote, that's all. Now I have a large paper to get out and not enough stories to fill it with. So unless you want to write a story about a pumpkin, you'll have to leave. Sorry."

He resumes writing.

"Okay," she says. He looks up. "I'll do it," she tells him. "I'll write about the pumpkin." She figures the longer she sticks around the more likely she is to earn his trust. Besides, she likes writing and it might even be fun.

A deadline is a deadline, Norman decides. He also decides that she's not only cute - okay, not relevant - but in spite of whatever issues she may have she seems to be quite smart. Maybe even capable. If she doesn't write well he'll fix it; if she does he saves time.

Pointing to a computer he hands Casey his notes and tells her to keep it simple and use the five Ws of news writing: who, what, when, where and why. "Have fun with it," he says, adding that "a pumpkin is a vegetable."

"I know that," she replies. "What else would it be?"

"I need ten colorful paragraphs."

"It's a pumpkin, not a national disaster."

"Ten."

Casey sits.

9.

Riley is walking down Venture Road, the street he lives on, he's a block from his home. He stops, puts Keeley's sandwich down, picks up a rock and goes into the classic baseball relief pitcher's stance. Vigorously shaking off the first imaginary sign, he checks the imaginary runner; he accepts a second imaginary sign, nods his head and delivers an imaginary pitch. A fastball. The rock hits a Stop sign with a resounding 'thwack' and two Stellar Jays in a nearby tree squawk and fly off.

"Steeerike three," Riley bellows. "The big guy from the little town K's another. Yes!" A fist pump and he dances over to pick up his sister's food and start the final block home. He walks along in the warm summer evening thinking about how cool it was to met a real detective, though she wasn't what he thought a real detective would be like. He is almost there.

Riley abruptly stops.

Mouth-agape, he drops the bag with the sandwich and stares at his yard, almost unable to believe what he sees. Or doesn't see. "Talk about a home run," he mutters.

The Miller yard is empty, their home gone.

Riley runs to the front of the yard and stares at the broken slats of the gate and the crushed white picket fence. Flower boxes with their hydrangeas and dirt spilling out are strewn about, one box sits on the road. Riley picks it up and, in a daze, puts it back into the yard. He notices tire marks on the lawn.

Approaching from the other direction come Agnes and Margaret, each carrying a bowling bag. "Did you sell your home?" Agnes asks.

Riley slowly shakes his head. "No. I mean I don't know...I don't know what happened," he mumbles. "It was here when I left this morning and now it's gone. I think I better get my brother."

He runs off.

At that moment, not far out of town, a black Cadillac follows a motor home down the highway alongside of Lake Still Waters. Keeley Miller is still in her room inside of the motor home and naturally she is afraid and very unhappy. She is also angry with her oldest brother.

"Norman," she yells out. "You PROMISED! NORRMMMANNN!!!

10.

It's early the following morning on Venture Road in the town of Still Waters, British Columbia. Cheerful birds sing and it is a bright day that once again promises to be hot. The Miller family yard now lacks a home but does not lack occupants for on the patch of ground the home sat upon for 20 years are two clumps in sleeping bags; inside of those sleeping bags are the Miller brothers.

They did not sleep much.

Upon finding their home gone, Riley ran to the newspaper office to tell Norman and together they ran to their yard, Casey following. When Norman saw there was no longer a home to go home to and that his sister Keeley was gone, he collapsed to the ground and tears ran down his cheeks. After a short time he stood and took to pacing about the yard, moaning over and over again that Keeley had been stolen.

For the longest while Riley simply stood near the apple tree, stunned. For her part, Casey did not want to intrude on their grief and stayed in the background and no attention was paid to her. After a while she discreetly took photographs of what was cleary a crime scene in case she may need them during the investigation, the one she was determined to conduct.

After Riley ran off, Margaret called Cpl. Harvey Kwong, head of the three-officer local RCMP detachment. Then she sat with Agnes upon their porch and watched the proceedings, filming only briefly, for they, too, did not want to intrude upon the grief the Miller brothers were experiencing.

When Cpl. Kwong arrived he quickly determined there were grounds for an Amber Alert and radioed in his request. Throughout that process he did his best to settle Norman. His two officers were on a call a little ways out of town so Cpl. Kwong told Norman he was needed to help canvas the neighbourhood and so must calm down. Norman did calm down, to a degree, and was able to help with knocking on doors.

Harvey, his first name being the one he insists locals use, canvassed down one side while Norman and Riley canvassed down the other, with Casey following the brothers and hovering near doors, offering the occasional question. There was very little information to gather as either people were not at home or unaware the motor home was even gone. The only person who saw anything was Tammy Lightbody from three doors down. Surprised, and secretly happy, to see it exit the neighbourhood, Tammy told Harvey she thought the Millers had at last decided to build a real house. She has three young children, all boys, and two were inside on their own at the time and she was in such a hurry to get inside herself ("I was worried they were breaking things or urinating on the cat") she didn't notice who was behind the motor home's wheel. She did hear Keeley yell Norman's name but thought nothing of it.

"Keeley can be a yeller," she told Harvey.

When the other two officers arrived they did a thorough examination of the yard for clues and took police photos. It was obvious the motor home had been driven through the fence and away, but beyond that they learnt very little. The investigating and clean-up of the flower boxes and debris took until midnight.

Harvey spoke to Casey, in particular he wanted to know why she had come to Still Waters and if she had brought anyone with her. Her answers were vague and he said he'd need to speak with her further the following day.

He told the brothers he had sent out an APB to go along with the Amber Alert and promised everything was being done to find their sister. He suggested they try to get some sleep.

Norman insisted he and Riley stay in their yard, wanting to be there in the event Keeley returned in the night. It took a long while before either was able to sleep and Norman only did so fitfully; he dreamt the newspaper office was flying, with him at his desk trying to write a story about a kidnapped pumpkin. In this dream he promised the pumpkin he would not carve it but he broke his promise and gave the pumpkin a sad face.

It is 7:30 a.m. and in the Miller yard an alarm is sounding; it is Casey Collier's phone, she is standing over the lump that is Norman and, in order to wake him, directing her phone toward his ear. He stirs. She turns off her alarm. Norman opens one eye and then, realizing someone is there, sits bolt upright.

"Keeley?"

"No. Sorry. Just me," she replies. "Time to get up."

"Oh Christ," he waves her away with his hand.

"I gather you're not a morning person."

"No, I'm just not an 'enjoys being annoyed after his sister and home disappear' person."

"I'm sorry. I'm only trying to help."

"Yeah," he sighs. "Give me a moment."

Casey is anxious to get going on her first case but, though she can hardly contain herself, she tries keeping quiet, doing her best to give Norman a moment to think and compose himself.

Norman looks up at the sky. He sighs again. The weight of what has transpired is a lot to bear. What should he do? How should he react? He doesn't know.

Casey can be still no longer and seeks to move things forward. "I slept in that park by your office," she says.

"Bluewater Park."

"Hard bench but I survived. We need an action plan."

"Who said anything about we?"

"Do you have any idea where we should start?"

"I can't think straight," Norman says. "It's hard to believe all this. I hardly slept."

"That's understandable. Look, I have to say something here: there is a role for us to play in this and I urge you not to become immobilized by anxiety and fear. Not to leave everything to the RCMP. Having said that, we should start by talking to that officer. Something might have come up overnight."

At last Norman sits up; he looks over to his brother, sleeping nearby. "Riley, up, wake up."

A hand reaches out from Riley's sleeping bag to grab his shorts. "Yeah," Riley mutters, putting his shorts on while still inside the sleeping bag. Out he gets now, standing and pulling his runners on, half-hopping about on one leg to do so.

Norman tells him to put the sleeping bags into the shed. Riley needs a place to pee, pointing out that the bathroom "doesn't seem to be where it was yesterday. Or anywhere."

Norman slept in his suit pants and undershirt and squirms out of his sleeping bag to grab the rest of his suit. He'd hung his shirt, jacket and tie on the branch of a tree but it all fell to the ground and everything is wrinkled. He tells Riley to go behind a tree but Riley wants none of that. Boys of 13 normally have no problem peeing outside but not with members of the opposite sex around; and not on the street they live on.

"What if she sees?" he says. "What if the neighbours see?"

"It's early, no one's outside. And if they didn't see something as big as our home getting stolen, I doubt they'll see your little –"

"Okay, I get your point." Riley goes behind a tree as Norman, while Casey patiently waits, puts on his shoes, picks up his notebook and stuffs it into a pocket.

"The ancient Greeks did what you're doing," Casey says, trying to be encouraging. "They would climb out of bed and just walk out the door and start their day."

"That is fascinating."

"They'd stop at a stand along the way, buy a bowl of oatmeal and keep walking while they ate."

"Oatmeal is not a good subject in our family," Norman tells her. He is out of the yard, Casey following. "I need to go to the office," he says. "I'll call Harvey from there."

Across the street, from an upstairs window, Agnes calls out; she tells Norman they are sorry they weren't at home when the thieves came. Margaret promises they will keep watch on the yard.

"Thank you," Norman replies. "When Keeley gets home we'll be over for bannock and tea." That is a tradition amongst the two families, to sit before a fire in Agnes and Margaret's living-room eating Agnes' bannock and drinking heaps of tea.

"Bless you," the ladies shout, in perfect unison.

Casey increases her pace to keep up with Norman. "It's good to get moving," she tells him. "The early bird gets the worm and all that."

Riley calls out from behind them: "That's a cliché."

"Riley isn't big on clichés these days," Norman tells her. "It's a phase."

"My point is that the best chance we have to find your parents and now your sister is to dive right into it."

"Another cliché," Riley calls out from the yard.

Norman stops and turns to Casey: "Why do you keep saying 'we'? There is no 'we' here. And I told you - my parents aren't missing."

"Right. Well, let's hope you're right."

"Like Harvey said last night, whoever did this probably meant to steal a mobile home and didn't expect anyone inside of it and they'll let her go today. I have to believe that or I'll go crazy."

"I don't want to press you at a difficult time but you have to do more than believe something," she says. "You do know that, right?"

"Sorry, but I can't deal with you right now."

"Okay. I get it. I'll pull back; for now." She smiles. Frustrated, Norman shakes his head and keeps moving.

Riley joins them and they walk three abreast. "I know we have to find Keeley but we didn't have supper last night and I'm starving. Could we stop for breakfast?"

They are passing by Keeley's food, abandoned the night before by Riley when he realized their home was gone. Norman picks it up and inspects the contents. "Lettuce, cheddar cheese and tomato. Should be fine."

He hands it to Riley. Riley pulls out the sandwich and has a bite. "Huh. It is." Takes another. "It's actually really good. I guess Alf is a good sandwich maker."

Norman says, "Nice to know your concern for your sister hasn't ruined your appetite."

Riley talks while chewing: "Know what? I bet Keeley will start complaining and they'll just let her go. I bet cash money that happens." Riley holds out the sandwich and offers a bite to his brother and Casey. They decline.

"I don't know who'd do this to us," Norman says. "We don't have enemies. I expect someone saw a chance to get a free home and went for it. Gypsies relocating and needing transportation maybe."

"They probably cased it out before Keeley moved in," Riley says. "Maybe they knew it was deadline day and thought we'd be at the office and it would be empty."

"That makes a certain sense," Norman says.

On the other side of the street an older man in a golf shirt and plaid shorts walks in the opposite direction. It is the town's former mayor, Crozier Rhodes, one term removed, and a past president of the Chamber of Commerce. Rhodes stops in front of a road sign.

"Look at this, Norman." he calls across the road. "Someone must have thrown something at this Stop sign. Dented it bad. Never used to see that in this town but by golly we're getting more and more like the big city every day." Riley tries not to look guilty. "Have your parents been found?"

Norman says, "They were never missing, actually. So no, they weren't found. They're fine."

Riley mutters, "So you say."

"Say, at the cafe this morning talk was you guys sold your home and are moving out of town. Selling the paper. Any truth to those rumors?"

"None. We're not going anywhere, Cro. Promise."

"Good. Glad to hear the Still Waters rumor mill is wrong yet again," Rhodes says. "We don't want to lose the best community newspaper in the region. What am I talking about? Best in the whole damn province." Rhodes waves and walks off.

Casey says, "Rumors start quick around here."

"Small town, people talk," Norman says.

"This will hit the news all over the province you know," Casey says. "Maybe even the country."

"I know."

"May I say something?"

"If it's helpful."

"Think about what I said last night. I mean wouldn't you say that what happened lends a note of truth to it?"

"A note of truth to what?"

It seems obvious to Casey. "That people are coming here to get revenge on your family."

"My parents write stories about bake sales and fire-smart work-shops. They don't have enemies. I write most of the political stories but they're balanced and I haven't had any real complaints. You just read that story that Riley wrote, which is not true, so you –

Riley says, "Yes it is."

" – stay out of this Riley – so you came here looking for a job. But there isn't one. Or there wasn't. Could you please let me think for a minute?"

"Okay. I'll shut-up."

"You said that earlier. It hasn't worked out so well."

She purses her lips and draws a zipper across them.

Riley says, "Non-verbal cliché."

They arrive at the familiar cross-walk and must cross to get to the newspaper office. There is traffic. Casey steps out ahead of the Miller brothers, she's in the cross-walk now, and confidently raises both hands; cars going in either direction stop and the way to cross is clear.

"She's pretty good," Riley points out.

"So she could have been a crossing guard," Norman says. "Big deal."

They cross.

Cpl. Kwong waits outside the Current office. A by-the-book officer, he's in his early-30s with short-cropped black hair and an understated manner; his primary break from police decorum that insistence that those he serves call him by his first name, believing it helps remove the distance people feel around officers. Nearing the end of a three-year rotation, he's from the small community of Horseshoe Bay and the rhythm of Still Waters suits him nicely. Small-town newspapers rely on police for information and police count on newspapers to get the word out to the community, so he knows the Miller family well.

Jack Smith doesn't show up until later in the morning so the office is empty as they file inside. Norman tells Riley to put the coffee on and sits at his desk and offers Harvey the seat across from him. Casey leans against the desk she wrote the pumpkin story in. Norman is desperately hoping Harvey has good news.

No such luck.

"I'm sorry but so far, nothing." Harvey begins. "The APB and Amber Alert got back sightings of motor homes heading both away from Vancouver and toward Vancouver. In summer the roads are full of them. Even older model homes like yours. No one in town or out of town has come forward to say they saw your home but maybe we'll get something now that the news is out."

Norman says, "It doesn't make sense."

"I still don't think this is about Keeley," Harvey says. "But if it is we should get a ransom demand today. Let's hope it's not and they find a safe place to let her go. But no matter what this is about, we're going to find her."

"She's super-annoying," Riley says, pouring water into a coffee pot. "So they'll probably just let her go."

"Riley, this is super serious, so enough of that kind of talk."

"Ms. Collier, last night you said you saw a black Cadillac in front of the family's motor home. Did you remember any more details? A part of the licence plate, if anyone was in the car?"

"I didn't look close. I should have. I think I saw people but I didn't get a real look at them. Just heads."

Norman says, "Someone other than Tammy must have seen something. Like noticed complete strangers driving off with our entire home. Did you hear from any neighbours who weren't around when we canvassed?"

"Both the Whites and the LaRoys are out of town. The Cadillac your friend here saw is the only clue we have and it would be a better clue if she had more details."

"I've only just met her," Norman says. "She is not my friend."

"Thanks for the ringing endorsement."

Harvey looks at Casey. He is suspicious of her showing up to ask about the Miller family right before the motor home and Keeley disappear. But she was with Norman when it was driven off and he asked around and she was seen getting off the bus alone so she's not much of a suspect. Last night she told him she belonged to the Canadian Association of Private Detectives and promised to fax him a copy of her licence this morning.

"I'm still waiting on your fax."

"I'll get on that."

"And I'm not forgetting what you said about someone being interested in that story of Norman's in the paper and looking to come here."

"That would Riley's story," Norman points out. Riley rolls his eyes.

Casey regrets telling Harvey she overheard anything but she had to explain why she came to be there. She wants a job, she wants to solve the case, and giving away information is not in her own best interest. Naturally she is concerned for Keeley but she doesn't know who stole the home or if what she heard had anything to do with it. It doesn't make sense to tell the police about bugging a pay phone, an illegal act, if she isn't sure there's a connection. She decides to continue to be less than forthcoming.

"Well like I said last night someone may be angry with the Millers for something in the past," she says. "But I don't know what and I don't know who or how angry they are. When I say it like this, well, I have to admit it doesn't sound like much and probably even sounds a little suspect."

Harvey says, "It doesn't sound like much, no. And yet it was enough to get you to take a bus here and offer your services."

Norman jumps in, "She has an overactive imagination. I mean everybody loves my parents, you know that. The most controversial story my Dad has written in years was about whether a fruit stand should be allowed to open next to the general store. They read, hike, make their own pasta, practice yoga and cheer for the Canucks. That's about it."

Harvey looks at Casey. "I'll ask you direct: how did you get your information?"

This is the question Casey didn't want to answer last night and was glad that just when it seemed Harvey was about to ask it, his officers showed up to distract him. She's ready for it now.

"I overheard a conversation outside a restaurant, but I wasn't close to the speakers and didn't see them," she says. "I thought I heard the name Miller." She veers next into outright lying. "Then I happened to read Norman's story and I made a connection and wondered if the missing parents might be who they were talking about. But maybe the connection doesn't exist, in which case it's just a coincidence I was here when the home was stolen. I'd still like to help though."

Norman tells Harvey, "I knew she didn't know anything. It's hard to understand what she's saying sometimes. She talks in circles."

Finished with putting on the coffee and opening windows, Riley pulls himself onto his favorite place on the front counter, "She does have a lot of hyperbole going for her, Norman," he says. "How's that for a cool word?"

Harvey stares at Casey a few moments. "I am not sure what to think about you," he finally tells her. "But if you're withholding information and I find out, I will charge you."

"I get that." Casey smiles. "But I'm not and I don't know who might have done this. If I did, I'd tell you."

"Let's move on," Harvey turns to Norman. "Your neighbours said your family used to have, one of them used the word drills. You'd open the front gate and everybody would get in the motor home and it would start, but not move. What was that about?"

"It was so we'd be ready," Riley offers.

"Ready for what?"

"To go," Riley says. "That's all Mom and Dad told us: to practice getting ready."

"Norman?"

"They were like fire drills. For years I thought every family did it."

"You don't feel those drills have anything to do with what Ms. Collier said about someone being angry at your family?"

"No, I think my parents were worried about a nuclear war or environmental disaster. If they don't have something to worry about they're not happy." Harvey looks skeptical. "And the motor home was about economics. It was all they could afford after buying the paper. For years it was the three of us but with Riley and Keeley it got crowded so they moved with Keeley into the apartment here. And we stopped having the drills."

"Agnes and Margaret hadn't seen Keeley since your parents left," Harvey says. "Why is that?"

"Sometimes she won't come out of her room, that's all."

"Okay." Harvey stands. "I'm getting a list of Cadillac owners in BC. I'll be coordinating with a Det. Sgt. Reg Lambert of Vancouver 42 division; you can call either of us whenever you like. In the meantime – be careful."

After Harvey leaves, Norman checks the messages on the paper's landline as Riley goes over to pour coffee. "Sorry. No coffee yet," Riley says. "Forgot to plug it in."

Norman tells him to forget it. "There are over a dozen messages from media asking about Keeley. The phone will be ringing all day," he says. "No sense trying to work. Let's go back to the yard and wait."

He and Riley head for the door.

Casey follows.

11.

Still Waters is not a large town, population at the last census was 2,578, though others live in rural areas nearby and do much of their shopping and socializing in town. It's friendly and there are many organizations to join, such as the arts umbrella, the nature club and the heritage society; there's even a juggling club. The Current keeps everyone connected and James and Lana's philosophy is simple: cover news, do a weekly profile and make sure to get plenty of names and photos in every issue. There are stories about municipal politics and land use issues, about bake sales and spelling bees, along with sports stories and articles reporting local accomplishments, however minor (a big orange vegetable might get ten paragraphs, for example). The paper has a column called The Slow Lane Chronicles in which Norman, James, Lana or Riley, twice now Keeley, takes a walk in the community and writes about whoever and whatever they encounter. Not just humans make it into The Slow Lane, there have been stories about dogs, cats, horses, a goldfish and a family of mule deer. Once a week the back page is devoted to seven photos taken at local events or just random shots of people. They are an interesting if often esoteric grouping of citizens, like the time Norman's back page was seven pictures of locals named Mike; a week later it was seven locals named Nancy. Riley once took photos of seven locals who were fans of the Vancouver Canucks and Keeley did seven pictures of friends who thought boys were stupid, though Norman used 'not as smart as girls' in place of stupid. That went over big. The fact the paper gets enough advertisers in a small town to publish twice weekly is a testament to their success and every local business advertises in it because most everyone reads it, cover to cover.

The Current is one of the reasons people know one another in Still Waters and because they know one another they often notice strangers. So when Benjie and Jerry drove down Main Street on the morning after stealing the motor home and Keeley they were seen by some as visitors. Unlike the night before they drove right into the downtown area at a busy time. Benjie thought it foolish and unnecessary and, while hesitant to be disloyal, worried they were going too far in the pursuit of revenge. Their ministry was crumbling and they'd have to relocate and it was the fault of a reporter who once wrote for a paper in Vancouver and now owned the paper in this town, all of that he knew. But with the taking of the motor home that reporter had lost his home much like Reverend Broom lost his. Didn't that satisfy the Bible's eye for an eye? Benjie prayed they would let the girl go and get on with the move to Guyana. He is not optimistic, however.

"Jerry," he says, as they drive down Main Street. "It is a fundamental principal of bank cards that you don't need to go to the actual bank the card was issued at. We can take that card to a machine in another town, or for that matter another province."

"So what?"

"So someone might have seen us last night. You know? Last night when we stole a motor home and a human being? I mean we are the definition of conspicuous."

"Hey. Don't call me names. I am not coniferous, or whatever you said I was."

"You're joking, right?" Benjie pretty much knows Jerry isn't joking. "You know a coniferous is a type of a tree, right?"

"So you're calling me a tree?"

"I didn't say coniferous, okay? I said con-spic-u-ous."

"You're the one slept outside with trees instead of inside. Whad'ya sleep outside with trees for anyhow?"

"Because it was beautiful and because I wanted to distance myself from the kidnapping of a little girl."

"Well you're part of it, no getting out of that." Jerry pulls into a parking space in front of the bank and shuts off the car. "You know, you don't talk smart like this around your father; you obey him, like a son should. I even seen you bow down to him."

"I have a black belt. We show respect to our elders by bowing. He likes that."

"I know all about your belt and one of these days we're gonna see who is tougher: muscles and fists like I got or that martial arts shit you do. I look forward to that. But for now, wait here and try not to look suspicious."

Looking suspicious, Jerry climbs out. Enjoying playing the bigshot, he looks around, stares at locals passing by, adjusts his dark sunglasses and hikes up his pants. He sticks his head back in the open car window. "I'm going in," he says. Benjie gives him a mock salute and says, "Good luck, Captain." Jerry gives Benjie the thumbs up and walks off and into the bank.

From the other direction comes Jack Smith. Richard O'Farrell, who does maintenance at the newspaper and built the apartment in back of the office (he also installed Keeley's call button) has stopped on the sidewalk by the bank's entrance and is staring at the Caddy.

"Hey Jack, look at that Cadillac," he says as Jack walks up next to him. "Sure is a beautiful car. Two guys I never seen pulled up in it."

"They're great looking cars, I guess. But I wouldn't wanna pay for all that gas."

"Yeah, you got that right."

Jack goes into the bank. Jerry is at the only machine there is, using Norman's card, which he lifted from the motor home. It was a replacement card and Norman wrote the code on a piece of tape and stuck it on the back, figuring he'd get rid of the tape once he memorized the code. So the password is right there: 1289. Jerry finds $310 in the account and withdraws all but ten, flips the card into the garbage and leaves.

Watching him, Jack finds it odd someone would throw a card away like that and once Jerry is out the door he digs it out. Norman Miller? He hurries outside and looks both ways but can't see the guy. No, wait, Jack thinks he does see him, yeah, the guy behind the wheel of the Cadillac, backing up. The Cadillac drives off.

Jack stares at Norman's card.

12.

A few feet from where his home once stood, Norman sits alone in his yard anxiously going over a host of questions in his head. Like who would steal his sister? And is someone from the past really coming to harm his family? And what can he do about it all? He decides he should leave it to the RCMP and that the best thing he can do is wait for his sister right where he is.

Casey and Riley arrive with coffee. Casey hands Norman a regular with 2 percent milk and a carrot muffin with butter, which Riley said his brother orders every time he goes to Alf's Cafe. Norman has picked three apples and hands them out. They sit upon the ground.

Casey feels she should keep them talking and learn as much as she can about the family. She asks about the neighbourhood and what it was like growing up in a small town. Not surprisingly Norman doesn't feel very talkative but Casey presses on.

"Did I tell you I got pictures of the yard last night?" Casey says. "Took about a dozen."

"Why would we need pictures of the yard?" Norman says. "We know what it looks like."

"It's important to be thorough and cover all bases."

"She's a giant cliche-emitter," Riley says.

"Good use of the word emitter," Norman tells his brother. "But don't be rude to strangers. Or anyone."

Casey is undaunted. "I'm not exactly a stranger anymore," she says. Norman certainly feels she is but says nothing. "Oh, by the way, I checked at the bus depot. The next bus for the city leaves in forty minutes."

"So you're finally going home?" Norman asks.

'No, we're all getting on it."

Norman doesn't get on buses. Or go to Vancouver. In general he doesn't go places unless he can walk or ride his bike to get there. He also doesn't do well with last minute decisions.

"And why would we do that?" he asks. "Why would the three of us get on a bus to the city together?"

Riley looks to Casey. "Told you he wouldn't go for it."

Casey says, "Because we're going to the motor vehicle branch in Vancouver to get a list of Cadillac owners in the province of British Columbia."

"And why would we do that?"

"Because we can't get it any other way. We went to the library and while your brother knows his way around a computer he couldn't get the list online."

"You're not answering my question."

"So I phoned the motor vehicle branch and got the rigmarole about how that information isn't given to private citizens. Blah blah blah. You have to apply. More blah blah blah. It could take months."

"You still haven't answered me."

"So best to go plead our case to a real human. If we have to, we'll bribe someone. I have some cash on me."

"Are you finished?" Norman asks.

She shakes her head. "And if bribery doesn't work we'll steal the information. Okay. Now I'm finished."

"You really do have a mental health problem."

Riley says, "And she likes clichés."

Casey says, "Look, you never know until you try, right?"

"Told you," Riley says.

Norman shakes his head. "We don't need to do this. If there's a list I expect the RCMP have it already and they'll probably find the car by this afternoon."

"The way bureaucracy works it could take months. Besides, in detective work parallel investigations are quite common."

Norman says, "I've never even heard that phrase."

"Let me finish: isn't it obvious that if we don't know where to look we can't find her but if we identify the owner of the Cadillac we'll know where to look."

Norman is getting fed up. "Here's a problem I see with that: we have no idea what we're doing."

"We can learn," Casey says. "Look, if you want something done in this world – you have to do it yourself."

"Ouch," Riley moans. "One of the worst clichés ever."

Norman says, "Do you have any experience with kidnapping?"

"Yes. I studied tracking people and did well on the exam." Riley rolls his eyes. "And I know this: if you want something done the best way to be certain that it gets done, is to do it yourself."

"Which you just said already," Norman says.

Riley adds, "And which I pointed out is a terrible cliché."

"Well, clichés become clichés because they're true."

"That is also a terrible cliché."

"Okay, enough," Norman says. "Casey, I don't know you. And if

I did know you, how am I supposed to know I would *want* to know you? And have you thought about the fact the Cadillac may have nothing to do with this?"

"Why are you so negative?" Casey turns to Riley. "Why is he so negative?"

"I told you: the guy is aggressively passive. He also gets car sick, though we don't know for sure because he won't go in a car."

"I have so been in cars," Norman insists. "Occasionally."

"Almost never," Riley says. "And get this: besides a few family camping trips, Norman has never left Still Waters. Like never as in *never ever*."

Casey says, "Quite a resume, Norm. Maybe you should live in a box."

"I know what you're thinking," Norman counters. "But I am not a coward. If I thought going to Vancouver would help find Keeley, I'd be on the next bus. But I don't so I am going to stay right here at home, which happens to be where my sister knows she can find me."

"You don't have a home," Casey points out. "Sorry, but they took the whole thing. Remember?"

"You know what I mean."

A horn honks and a green pick-up truck drives up. Jack Smith gets out and moves into the yard, wide-eyed at seeing the empty space. Looking at the broken gate he realizes the motor home may have been stolen. James doesn't have enemies. Does he?

He's suddenly jolted by memories he's worked to keep away. Slowly walking toward Norman, he tells himself the empty yard could not be connected to the past, but the memories stab at him. He stops, stares, starts to speak but can't think of anything to say.

"Someone stole our home last night," Riley tells him, matter-of-factly. "We don't know who."

Norman says, "With Keeley inside of it."

Struggling not to show his anxiety over the memories he's now gripped by, Jack resolves to tell Norman what he came to tell him and not dredge up a past that is almost certainly not connected. Norman doesn't know about it and it's not time to tell him.

"No ransom demands," Norman is saying. "And there isn't much in the way of clues."

"I'm sorry to hear that. What does Harvey say?"

"Not a lot," Norman says. "Like I said there aren't any clues and no one saw whoever took it. He put out some alerts."

Jack thrusts out the bank card. "Here, this will seem anti-climatic but I found it. I don't know if it's related. This young guy, I've never seen him before, used it at the bank and then he just threw it in the garbage."

Casey snatches it. "This was on the floor of the motor home. I put it on the counter. The guy you saw must have taken it from there."

"Who is she?" Jack asks Norman.

"A deluded person." Norman grabs his card from Casey. "Casey, this is Jack Smith, he's a reporter at the paper. Jack this is Casey Collier, I'm not sure what she does."

"I'm a detective working the Miller case."

"See what I said about being deluded?" Norman looks at the card. "Got this two days ago; taped the passcode to the back. Stupid but with so many stories floating around inside my head I forget small things."

"Could you describe the man who had it?" Casey asks.

"White male, early 20s with short hair, stocky, tough-looking. There was another guy in the passenger seat; I think he had brown skin and wavy hair."

Casey asks, "What were they driving?"

"A black Cadillac. Older model."

She's excited. "Are you sure?"

"Yeah, stood out in his town."

Casey turns to Norman. "This can't be a coincidence. It's the same car and the same people. Your sister needs us. We don't wanna miss that bus."

Riley says, "Don't wimp out on me, Bro."

Norman sighs, closes his eyes. He thinks of his baby sister alone, frightened and surrounded by jerks. Keeley? Kidnapped? He has to find her, he has to try.

He says, "Jack, you'll have to finish getting this edition out on your own."

"Mostly just layout left. Shouldn't be a problem."

"This has hit the news so better write a story, take out the one about the firefighters, that can go next week. Just the basics, the motor home was stolen, Keeley is missing. Get a quote from Harvey." Jack nods.

Norman turns to his brother. "Riley, come on, we have a bus to catch."

"Yes!"

Norman and Riley walk out the yard.

Casey follows.

13.

The sign on the outside of the bus depot is a source of amusement for locals, the 'u' fell off years ago and was never replaced so it reads 'STILL WATERS B S DEPOT.' There are docks for two buses; one leaving for points east, it will make its way to Toronto, the other west to Vancouver. Casey, Norman and Riley stand beside the Vancouver bus, its engine warming. The sky is grey and it threatens to rain as the driver punches tickets and the passengers file on. After he and Riley hand over their tickets, Norman hesitates at the bottom of the stairs. He stares up at the bus and grimaces.

"What the matter?" the driver jokes. "You never been on a bus before?"

"That's right. This is my first time."

Riley gently pushes his brother forward and Norman sighs and slowly climbs the three steps. Riley is right behind.

Casey follows.

"See the guy in the wrinkled suit?" the driver asks as she hands him her ticket. "He's never been on a bus before."

"Just lucky I guess," she says.

At the back of the line-up, filming, are Agnes and Margaret. They feel they let their neighbours down by missing Keeley and the mobile home being taken and are trying to make it up by chronicling the brothers with even more zeal. From their window across from the Miller yard they heard the conversation about taking a bus to the city and decided if nothing else, an adventure would do them good.

"We may be getting old," Agnes had said, thinking about the lyrics from a song by her favorite artist, Muddy Waters. "But we got young-fashioned ways."

"We're not *getting* old," Margaret countered. "We *are* old."

Inside the Greyhound, Norman sits in back by a window, Riley next to him. Casey grabs the seat across the aisle. Norman checks the window signs to learn the procedure in the event of an accident. He fiddles with a lever and tests knobs.

"Careful," Casey, teasing him, leans across the aisle to say. "You're liable to fall out."

"I'm sure you'd follow me," he replies.

"Why bother?" Riley pipes up, "If there's an accident, you either live or die. Simple."

"Should I ever fly on a plane remind me not to do it with you," Norman says.

"Fat chance of that, Bro."

"Isn't 'Bro' a cliché?" Casey asks.

Riley thinks. "Yeah. I guess. Thanks."

Agnes and Margaret are last on and sit behind the driver, who takes his seat and puts it into reverse and backs out. Norman hastily reaches for his seatbelt, mistakenly trying to jam his shoulder strap into Riley's clasp. Riley grabs it and does the job for him.

"Like I said, it doesn't matter: you live or die."

"Yes, I believe you mentioned that."

It begins to rain.

14.

Jerry's impromptu decision to steal the motor home left him without a plan and with nowhere to go. Taking it into Vancouver would not work, far too conspicious to leave on a city street.

Earl drove long-haul trucks before becoming the number one disciple of Reverend Vernon Broom and had no trouble operating the motor home. A nervous Benjie rode shotgun, frequently calling back to the girl in the room that everything would be okay. In truth Benjie didn't know what was going to happen and did not think everything would be okay.

Not far down the highway, driving in the direction of Vancouver, Jerry, ahead in the Cadillac, took a turn-off and Earl followed. Jerry made another turn and another and they were rumbling down a country road. No pavement, lots of ruts and bumps. But there was no traffic and they couldn't be seen from the highway.

The motor home soon began to sputter and clunk so Earl steered into a clearing near the third fairway of the Crippen Valley Golf Course. He didn't know if it was out of gas or there was a mechanical problem but either way, the Miller home's return to road operation was over. Thanks to bushes and trees it wasn't visible to golfers, or to anyone. It was a good hiding spot.

When he drove into Still Waters all Jerry intended to do was what he was told, find the Miller home. He pulled up to a pedestrian, said he was a cousin of James Miller's from Alberta and she gave him directions. Upon seeing it was a mobile home Jerry decided to steal it. Finding the girl inside was a welcome bonus and when he called his father to tell him what he'd done, Jerry got a big helping of the approval he was forever seeking.

"You saw an opportunity and put your mind to it," his father said. "You've done the ministry proud."

At that time, Reverend Broom was holed up in a motel in Vancouver telling himself to be patient. He believed the missing couple from the story Earl saw were alive for he did not think God would bring the reporter back into his life only to deny him the pleasure of his revenge. He would turn up and, thanks to Jerry, the man had now lost his home, as he, Broom, had lost his, and he must worry about losing his daughter. But why stop at that, Broom mused?

Here's this: Reverend Broom considered the stories James Miller wrote many years ago not only began the series of failures that lead to the loss of his home but also to the loss of his congregation, his disciples, what he considered his children. He had once failed to get his eye for an eye and the reporter disappeared. This time Reverend Broom intended to succeed, and brilliantly.

"Next," he told Jerry over the phone. "We get the sons."

He told Jerry there would soon be a description of the motor home in the news so even if it could be fixed it must stay hidden. He instructed his son to settle down for the night then pick him up in the morning.

As for Jerry's prisoner, Keeley had no phone and no data for her laptop so even if she knew where they were, which she didn't, she could not have told anyone. Benjie found food in the cupboards and offered to pass her in some. She told him to shut-up.

Jerry laughed about that. "See what you get for being nice?" he asked Benjie.

Benjie stayed out of the way of his father and Jerry. He preferred it outside anyhow, where he could sit amongst the trees and think. It was getting dark when they clunked into the clearing and any golfers still on the course had long played past the third hole and the land was still. Only rarely did Benjie get the chance to spend time in nature and while disturbed about the events he was involved in, the surroundings helped him to feel a measure of peace.

This was not the first time the Reverend and his father sought revenge. He thought of the time Reverend Broom excommunicated a member of the congregation, the manager of a car-rental business who refused to rent trucks to the congregation for free. Reverend Broom had Earl, Jerry and Benjie smash windows at his place of business. Such acts made Benjie feel dishonorable and that first night in the clearing he strained to think of a way out of this while still obeying his mother's dying wish that he remain loyal to his father. He feared he would either have to lose his father or do things he did not believe he should do.

He slept on a soft piece of ground in a thicket near the motor home, falling asleep while gazing at the stars. Jerry slept in Norman's bed while Earl slept in the chair next to Keeley's room.

It was the next morning that Jerry and Benjie drove into Still Waters to empty Norman's bank account; Jerry did not tell his father he was doing so but was again hoping to gain approval for thinking on his own. After he withdrew the money from Norman Miller's account they drove to a Vancouver lumber store where they bought deadbolts for Keeley's room and a Generac 5500 watt portable generator. They also had a wooden traffic barrier made that read 'Road Closed: Flooding.' It had been four days since the storm but Reverend Broom wanted the sign to keep motorists from venturing down the road leading to the motor home. At an electronics store they bought a security camera and at a grocery market a supply of food was purchased. Along the way they heard a news report about a missing 10-year-old named Keeley Miller. Jerry laughed and hooted. Benjie felt sick.

Once they had everything they picked up Reverend Broom from his motel. The Reverend considered going back to his repossessed home to get his dog but decided placing the flooding sign was a priority and they started back for the mobile home.

A glutton for approval, Jerry could hardly wait to boast about paying for the sign with money from Norman Miller's bank account. He boasted that they "went right into that crummy town" to use the card at the "same bank it must have been from."

"That was foolish," his father scolded. "Someone may have seen you last night and noticed the car. Do not return to the town again."

Oops. Jerry was stung by that and tried to regain his father's approval by telling him the girl was mouthy and asking if he could "teach her a lesson." Benjie was relieved when Reverend Broom told him to leave the girl alone.

"It's more important to find the brothers," Reverend Broom said. "I lost my family so he must lose his."

"Only how do we get the brothers if we can't go back into the town?" Jerry asked.

"The Lord works in mysterious ways," his father said. "He will show you how."

Earl stayed at the motor home that first morning, guarding Keeley and reading an Elmore Leonard novel he found by Riley's bed. He passed her in a box of juice and a tuna sandwich and explained they did not yet have a generator so the juice wasn't cold.

She called him a jerk.

Curious about her, he stuck his eyes up to the slot. Light streamed in through the opening but he couldn't see much. He pressed his eyes closer to the slot.

"Let's have a look at you," he said.

On the other side, Keeley was looking through the slot and saw Earl's eyes peering back at her. She grinned and moved her head back. She held up her right hand, spread two fingers apart, about two inches, and then quickly jabbed them through the slot. Bingo!

Earl recoiled, screaming and clutching at his eyes as he danced about the small space, bashing into walls and knocking over the chair. It took a minute for the pain in his eyes to subside but finally he was able to pick the chair back up and sit himself back down.

He was angry but also impressed. "She's got more spunk than my boy does," he muttered to himself. "That's for damn sure."

He smiled. "Not that it'll do her any good."

15.

The rain is pouring down as Norman Miller looks out the window of the bus; they have passed out of rural areas and been through the suburbs and are exiting the highway, the Vancouver bus depot minutes away.

Norman spent part of the trip dozing and the rest staring out the window and thinking about phobias, a subject he had recently read a magazine article on. He wondered if he had agoraphobia, an anxiety disorder characterized by the fear of being in situations that may cause panic, or enochlophobia, the fear of being in large crowds. In the end, he reasoned he probably had a touch of both. He did not know why he was the way he was but reasoned his childhood was a suspect.

He was more affected by his upbringing than he let on to Harvey. Growing up in a motor home and forever preparing to escape if something bad happened, he never knew what, did not create a bold outlook on life or lead to much in the way of bravado.

He thought how that atmosphere of uncertainty may explain his personality but he had no explanation for Riley's. Riley had courage and acted quickly and their parents had trouble keeping up with him. He was relentlessly bold. Norman sometimes found himself wishing he had paid more attention to his little brother: he might have learned something.

After they pull off the Trans-Canada, Norman looks at the immensity of the buildings in Vancouver. He's seen images and film footage of cities but finds being physically in one daunting.

Riley, who visited Vancouver on school trips and to play hockey – Norman never played sports and was excused from school trips – is on his tablet and pays no attention. Casey pokes Riley and asks him to switch seats. He whispers that he doesn't want to because earlier in the trip he saw the guy next to her digging a finger around inside of his nose.

"Well as long as he doesn't try picking at yours, Riley," she whispers back. "Besides, he's sleeping now." They make the switch.

Casey settles in next to Norman. "What do you think of the city so far?"

"I don't know," he says, avoiding the question. "I'm just looking out a window."

"Come on, first impression."

"Lots of people and a lot of noise. The buildings look dirty. You're staring at me."

"You're disturbed somehow."

"What? You mean as in mentally disturbed? You're calling me mentally disturbed?"

"No. Sorry. I meant that you seemed disturbed about something."

"Well, my sister being kidnapped is kind of disturbing, wouldn't you say?"

"Of course. Sorry. I meant about the trip we're taking."

"Let's just say I'm apprehensive. Are we nearly at the bus depot?"

"Yeah. Look, I gotta ask: how did you reach adulthood without experiencing a bus? And you avoid cars. Is that a syndrome?"

"I've been in cars. On family trips, a few times." Norman looks away. "It's different in a small town. I have no need for buses. I own a bike and I have two feet. I use them."

"I shouldn't analyse you. I'll stop."

"That would be nice."

"Oh. Hey. There is something I better tell you. It might come as a shock but you should know that Miller is not your real last name."

Norman turns his head toward her. "Could you repeat that please?"

"Your surname. It's not Miller. Like the name Miller wasn't originally your family's name."

"What are you talking about?"

"I don't what it is, but I do happen to know the letter it begins with."

"I will indulge you on this," Norman says. "You say my real surname is not Miller, but you don't know what my real surname is, but you *do* know the letter it begins with. Have I got all that right?"

"Your real surname begins with the letter 'h.'"

"Casey, do you find it hard to believe that I find you hard to believe?"

"No, I believe you."

Riley leans over from across the aisle, "We're here."

The moment the three walk out of the Vancouver Bus depot the rain stops and out comes the sun. Agnes and Margaret have slipped out behind them and as stealthily as they can manage follow from the other side of the street. Norman is busy being overwhelmed, Casey is busy watching Norman and Riley is busy enjoying the sights, so the two go unnoticed.

Margaret begins to film.

The Pacific Central Station in Vancouver is an immense concrete building erected not long after World War I, a grand structure with a vast lawn laid out in front. Norman is pleased with the touch of nature and as they make their way across the lawn he's happy to find there are only a handful of people on it; he thought every street in the city core would be teeming with humans. He looks to his right and stops, staring at the massive parking lot off to the side of the station; that's more cars in one place than he has ever seen. Casey explains that commuters come from all over the region and park there then walk or take transit the rest of the way to their jobs. That is not a surprise to Norman, he's heard about commuting of course, but he is still taken aback to see hundreds of cars all parked together.

They cross the lawn on to Hastings, one of Vancouver's busiest streets and not its most presentable, passing as it does through a hard-luck part of town. Norman is spooked by the cars and bustle and all the people. Most of those around him wear ragged clothing, many are slumped against doorways, and even in a wrinkled and older suit Norman feels overdressed. In this world normalcy has a different look.

At a cross-walk, a woman shoves by Norman, waving an arm in the air as she yells for a cab; when one screeches to a halt she hops in and it speeds off. Casey asks Norman if he's okay and he tells her he's "fine, thank you very much."

Despite having no map, no phone and no experience in a city, Norman reasons he does have skills and should be able to find the motor vehicle branch without relying on Casey. He sees a man with long gray hair wearing a t-shirt with a drawing of the universe and an arrow pointing to a dot representing the Earth; a caption reads: 'You Are Here.' The man looks gentle somehow, if dishevelled.

"Excuse me," Norman says to the man. "Can you tell me where the downtown motor vehicle branch is?"

The man looks down to his chest and points to the arrow on his t-shirt, the arrow that in turn points to the drawing of the universe and the dot that represents the Earth.

"Relatively speaking," the man says. "I'd say you're pretty much there already."

"I see what you mean," Norman replies, backing away. "Thanks. for your help." Norman tells Riley to stay near and waits for the light to change.

Cross-walks are, of course, not Norman's strong suit, and Vancouver's are far more challenging than anything he encounters in Still Waters. Mesmerized by the traffic, he fails to see the light change and so remains standing while others hustle past him and make their way across the road.

Casey taps him on the shoulder. "See the little stick man with his limbs moving?" she asks. "He's trying to tell you something."

Looking pointedly at her, as if to say 'watch me', he steps boldly onto the road, doing so at the moment a car turns into the cross-walk. The driver slams on the brakes and honks; Norman jumps back onto the curb.

"He came around too fast," he says.

"The way you cross streets it'll take you months to get there," Casey says as they finally cross. "If you live."

"You must have a family," Norman says. "Why not go and visit them?"

Casey walks in the direction of the motor vehicle branch. She stops. "You know what? It's all the way up Main to Carol Street and then over to Georgia. I think we better jump on a city bus."

"My first bus ride is enough for one day, thank you."

"It's a long walk."

"Norman likes walking," Riley points out.

"I prefer it in fact."

"Okay, walk it is then. Let's get started." They set off walking. "Now what was I saying?"

Norman says, "Not much I expect." Norman realizes that was a little rude. "Sorry. I don't remember."

"Oh, I remember. You asked about my family." A voice in her head reminds her detectives shouldn't reveal personal details to clients. She decides to ignore it.

"I'm an only child," she says. "I was adopted from China. One of those. Though as you can see, Vancouver has a lot of people who look like me. My parents are white. They decided to adopt in their 40s and there was only me and them. But if you want the ugly truth – "

"Which I'm not sure I do, actually."

" – they kind of abandoned me. Not when I was little. When I graduated high-school they sent me to Europe on my own. Or they offered a choice between what's called a 'heritage trip' to China, or one to Europe. I've been to China and it didn't work out, right? So I picked Europe. I backpacked. Worked at a youth hostel in Scotland, spent a week with gypsies in Romania, I crashed a motor scooter on the Greek island of Leros."

Norman says, "That sounds a lot more like a gift than abandonment."

"Yeah only when I got back they'd moved to Truro, Nova Scotia. You can't get much farther away and still remain in the country. We text. People don't use the phone anymore. Anyhow, that's the story of my family."

Norman isn't sure how to respond. He can't imagine being without his family and feels lousy she was abandoned by her biological family and adopted one. He suddenly has an impulse to give her a hug.

He resists.

"That's unfortunate," he finally says. "But I expect they miss you and I bet it had to do with work."

"You're right actually. Or so they claim. They're both geologists. There's a government research project out there. But they could have kept working here."

"I also bet they'd like you to move to Nova Scotia."

"Haven't asked. But not to worry. I'm the independent type."

They walk on, in silence.

Falling behind, Riley finds walking in a big city without a teacher or coach telling him to stay with the group exhilarating. Norman and Casey lose him two blocks from the bus depot but find him looking in the window of a lingerie store, staring at a female manikin in a string bikini. Norman moves him along but a block further Riley sneaks off into a variety store.

"Do you have the Financial News Weekly?" he asks the clerk.

"No, sorry."

"How about the Atlantic Monthly Business Review? It comes from out of the East."

"Sorry, no, we don't have that, either."

"Huh. Blomberg Business Daily?"

"Nope."

"Just gimme a Hustler then." The clerk turns and grabs a Hustler from the shelve but when he turns back, Norman is there shaking his head. "He's only 13," he tells the clerk. "Not funny, Riley."

"You told me to keep reading."

"Move along or I'll club you one."

"You're a young male entering the prime of your life," Riley says as they exit the store. "Those magazines have pictures of women. What's not to like?"

"I like women all right, but those magazines aren't always respectful."

"Prude."

They are passing by Casey's apartment and she stops to point out the window she sits and looks out at the world from. She tells them about the people she shares the building with. Norman quickly decides it is not a place he could live, people piled upon one another in boxes. She is telling them about her eccentric British neighbour when none other than Philip walks unsteadily out of the building, lugging a full set of golf clubs.

"Well well, what do we have here?" Philip bellows. He hiccups. "The ravishing phone booth queen. I see you've found new friends. Am I being replaced?"

"I didn't know you golfed, Philip," Casey says.

"Thought I'd try to fit in with the urban North American lifestyle," he says. "Here, watch this." He puts down his golf bag and pulls out a three-wood to demonstrate his swing; as he propels the club back it knocks over his bag, strewing clubs about the ground. Turning to pick them up, he trips over the bag and goes down. "Oops." Laying on his back in a heap of golf clubs – he hiccups.

"Good luck with that," Casey says.

"Hiccuping is cliché for a drunk," Riley tells Philip. "It's also pathetic."

"You shouldn't make sport of the unfortunate," Philip is back up on his feet. "What do they teach children in Canadian schools anyhow?"

Riley says, "Also your swing has a hitch."

"You're a golfing expert?"

"I drive balls from our office to the fountain in Bluewater Park. I can hit the water four out of five times."

"How nice for you." Philip is picking up his clubs.

Casey says, "Bye bye, Philip. Let's go." As Casey and the brothers walk off, Philip rushes up behind Norman, grabbing him. "Mister Canadian-with-Long-Hair, I gather that you are my ri – (hiccup) – val for her affections then, are you?"

"Me? No. Not at all. I don't even like her."

"Nice suit but it is rather wrinkled."

Norman keeps moving. As Riley walks by, Philip grabs his arm and pulls him to the side. "Hey, kid, I have some advice for you: see that phone booth on the other side of the street?" Riley nods. "Don't use it, ever."

Riley notices Agnes and Margaret standing near the phone booth. The two are filming. He waves.

Casey walks back and yanks on Riley's arm. "Have a nice day, Philip." She tugs Riley along.

"I'll be fine on my own," Philip says. "You folks go right ahead then."

"He said not to use the phone booth across the street," Riley tells Casey as they walk off.

"Just keep moving," she says. "He's from England."

As they continue walking, without Philip, Casey tells the brothers what she knows about buildings they pass. That hotel hosts a writer's festival; the best sushi is at that place, owned by a guy named Gary whose daughter plays hockey; a nightclub on the lower floor in another building was gutted by fire, everyone got out thanks to the screechings of an orange cat named

Booboo.

Now on Georgia St., they are in an area of concrete buildings, most of them devoted to government ministries. Massive concerte and steel structures, some modern, others old. Norman's head is on a swivel as he marvels at their size and design. Like a toddler, Norman stops and gawks, then rushes to catch up before stopping again. Casey enjoys his enthusiasm.

Reaching the building the motor vehicle department is in, Casey and Riley go inside and wait for Norman. When he arrives the revolving glass door entrance baffles him. Three aborted attempts before he makes it into the foyer, banging his head upon glass as he does.

Slightly wounded but ready for action.

16.

After putting up the 'Road Closed: Flooding' traffic barrier and driving to the motor home, Reverend Broom instructed his son on how to capture Norman and Riley Miller without going back into Still Waters. They were words Jerry had heard many times.

"Wait for God to show you the way," the Reverend Broom pronounced. "For He works in mysterious ways."

Benjie, who would be going with Jerry, doubted God wanted them to take hostages so he wasn't expecting any help from Him. He silently prayed that whatever Reverend Broom had planned no one would be hurt.

Benjie kept telling himself Broom and his father were not killers. His father went to prison, convicted of planting an explosive device that killed a woman and her son, and the Reverend was thought to have ordered him to do it. But Benjie believed they were innocent. The Reverend wasn't charged for lack of evidence and his father's conviction was based on a single fingerprint on the detonator. Meanwhile, the man the Reverend said committed the crime, Bud Clement, fled back to the U.S. and was never heard from again.

It was mid-morning by the time they left to go capture the Miller brothers without going into Still Waters. Jerry decided they would park outside the town and simply wait for them to drive by.

"God works in mysterious ways," he told Benjie. "He will bring them to us."

Benjie grimaced.

They sit in the Cadillac on a country road where it intersects with the Trans-Canada Highway. It is late morning and it is hot. Jerry alternates between staring at photos of Norman and Riley clipped from a copy of the paper found in the motor home and watching cars. He absently taps his gun on his knee.

Benjie is boiling and the water he brought has become too warm to quench his thirst. He is still reading Nietzshce but he's finding it hard to focus in the heat.

He doesn't have his phone for entertainment, he left it in the motor home. He cancelled his data because his father was right, it was taking up too much time. At the moment though he is stupefyingly bored without it.

"Shouldn't we develop a better plan?" he finally says. "I mean even if they were to drive by they'd be going so fast we wouldn't know it was them."

"I told you: God works in mysterious ways."

"That seems vague and it also seems like you're parroting your father."

"Did you call my father a 'parrot'?"

"No, Jerry, forget it. You know these brothers might only leave town once or twice a month, if at all. So the law of averages suggests we might be here a very long time."

"I don't give a shit about no law."

Benjie has spent enough time around Jerry to know conversation with him generally goes nowhere. But he is terribly bored and decides to keep trying.

"This book," he says, showing Jerry the cover. "This Nietzsche guy believed whatever we do we end up doing over and over again for eternity. That thought makes me uncomfortable with some of things you and I do. Do you ever feel that way?"

Jerry stares at Benjie. He doesn't like him. Never has. But he's stuck with him.

"I don't know nothing about that," he says. "But I do know these brothers gotta leave town sometime." Benjie wishes he hadn't bothered trying. "And unless you wanna end up in cement like Mister Clement, when the time comes you better do your job."

Benjie finds 'in cement like Mister Clement' an odd phrase, one Jerry has used before. "Where did you get that from?" he asks now. "Do you mean Bud Clement, the guy who probably killed that mother and son?"

"Never mind about that: just do your job."

Benjie goes back to being bored.

17.

At the motor vehicle branch, Norman takes ticket 238 and joins those already waiting. His plan is simply to ask at a counter for a list of Cadillac owners. As a reporter, he finds asking more often gains an answer and, regardless of what that answer is, it allows him to move forward. He does not expect the first official he asks to give him the list but is confident he'll be directed to someone who will. The flashing electronic counter on the wall tells him number 193 is being served and he begins doing the math. Riley beats him to it.

"There are 45 people ahead of us," Riley says. "We might be sitting here awhile."

Norman looks at the big-city people he is surrounded by. Seated near him are teenage identical twin girls, brown skin, talking animatedly, excited about getting their learners licence; a woman who appears to be their grandmother has a red dot upon her forehead. He tries to remember what that means but is distracted by a middle-aged ethnically Chinese woman in a surgeon's mask. He considers why and decides it must be due to a fear of contacting an air-borne virus. "Makes sense," he mumbles. Now his attention is taken by a middle-aged chubby white guy, bald on top, long straggly hair on the sides. The man is emphasizing a point to a pimply and pale-faced young man working a counter, pointing emphatically at a piece of paper and telling the young man the accident "wasn't my bloody fault." Norman feels uneasy about the encounter and is relieved when the agitated man stomps out.

Riley doesn't think his brother's approach will get them the information they need. Besides it's dull and Riley doesn't like dull. He makes his way to the elevators. He wears number 31 in hockey (a goalie, naturally) but there are only twenty floors. In baseball he wears number 10 and when the elevator arrives he pushes the button for the tenth floor.

Casey is skeptical Norman will get results by waiting for a long line of people to be served then simply asking a counter attendant to hand over the list. But at least he's doing something, more or less, and she decides motivating him to act is a secondary part of the job she's taken on. So progress is being made.

She asks a janitor what floor the records department is on and he tells her there are five consecutive floors making up that department, beginning at the tenth. When Casey steps off the elevator on the tenth she walks down the hallway and peers into offices where workers sit in cubicles and enter data. She hears a woman giving a series of admonishments to an underling and concludes anyone as bossy as she clearly is must be high up. She enters the woman's office.

She asks about obtaining a list. The woman, who wears a name-tag that says Florence, informs Casey the public is not given such lists without applying for one and she would need certain credentials to qualify. Casey asks, cajoles and flat-out demands, all to no avail.

"However," Florence tells her. "You are welcome to fill out this form and within a four-to-six-week period we will get back to you, unless, of course, we can't. Any further questions?"

"But I can't wait six weeks. A girl has been kidnapped. You might have heard about it or seen a story on the news this morning?"

"Dreadful, but the police can obtain the list easily enough. I simply can't break those rules for a private citizen."

"But six weeks? Isn't there something I can do to speed things up? Pay an extra fee? To you perhaps?"

"That would be an emphatic no," Florence replies. "Now thank you and good day."

On the way back down the hall, Casey passes a small office with an open door and hears a familiar voice call out "Hi." It is Riley, alone in there. He waves at her as she enters and then goes back to typing at a computer.

"What are you doing?" she asks.

"What do you think?' he says. "Using a computer to get a list of Cadillac owners. No one was here so I sat down."

On the screen is data. Riley points the cursor at the print menu and clicks. There's a whirring sound in behind Casey and she turns and watches one and then a second sheet of paper print out. Squeezing by her, Riley pulls out both sheets and has a look.

"Sure is a lot of Cadillacs in B.C."

"You mean that's it? You did it? You have the list?"

"Yup." Riley casually walks out the door.

"You know, I like you, Riley," Casey says, following. "I mean you're pretty darn cool."

"Tell that to my brother."

While they wait for the elevator, Casey pulls out her phone and snaps a photo of the list. It fills two pages and she thinks about how time-consuming investigating each name would be; there must be an easy way to narrow the list down. Harvey likely has a copy now and she realizes how badly she would like to find Keeley before he does. It occurs to her she is hoping to play hero to the Miller family and admits to herself that she enjoys being a part of Norman and Riley's world.

Up pops this embarrassing memory of being 11 or 12 and going on a vacation with neighbours, a couple from India who came to Canada as newlyweds, found success owning a grocery store and had a large family. She often played with a daughter her age, Rishi, and one year they invited her to go along on their summer camping trip to Cedar Point Provincial Park at Quesnel Lake. They bought her a rod and taught her fly-fishing and for a reason she can't fully remember they called her Chitra, a Hindi name; it was something to do with a picture she had once painted at their home. For two full weeks she was part of the pack, they treated her as family, she was even disciplined like the others. There was a racist incident, rednecks telling them to go back home and there she was with two of Rishi's brothers yelling back that they were Canadians and that they were at home, so there. She remembers this wonderful feeling of belonging. On the drive back she asked the mother, they travelled in two cars there were so many of them, if she could move across the street to their house and live with them. She cried when she was gently told no. The family moved to Victoria the following spring to open a clothing store and she never saw them again. They took a while to forget though.

Casey watches Riley as they ride down in the elevator and realizes she has only known the Millers a short time and yet were she to go back to her old life without them she would feel a sense of loss. She reminds herself not to get attached personally and that the most important thing is finding Keeley.

In the lobby Norman tells them there are now only twenty people ahead of them. "It won't be that long a wait, some people leave before their number comes up," he says. "And besides, people watching is fun."

"Well you got a whole city of people to watch," Casey says, taking Norman's ticket and dropping it in a waste basket. "Riley got the list. Come on, time for lunch and I know just the place."

18.

Riley is loving The Rainy Day Diner. He's only seen a jukebox once before and in their booth he flips through the playlist and puts on Steppenwolf's 'Born to Be Wild.' It's the first jukebox Norman has seen but when their food arrives he insists on keeping it off. The owner, Lindsay, offers Riley a free soda and Norman refrains from his anti-sugar speech and allows him to have it.

Here's this: against all odds the three have accomplished what they came to Vancouver to do and while they're still faced with the daunting task of finding Keeley, they are in decent spirits.

Initially the list is a magnet to Norman. As they wait for their food he looks at the names and wonders which one took Keeley. He wants to call them and ask if they have his sister locked up somewhere and when he finds the right one, beg them to give her back.

Casey points out that random phone calls would prove fruitless and with over 300 names on the list they need to find a way to narrow it down. She adds that "even if we called the right number they're hardly going to admit they have a kidnapped girl in their basement."

Norman grudgingly admits what she says makes sense and, easily defeated, soon begins to feel less enthusiastic about having obtained the list. A feeling of failure creeps into his psyche and a nervous sense of loss sits in the pit of his stomach.

He tries to put those feelings out of his mind by calling Harvey on Casey's phone. Harvey tells him he is optimistic it was a theft, not a kidnapping and believes the absense of a ransom demand means she will be let go.

Casey is curious and takes the phone and asks if the RCMP have a list of Cadillac owners. They do and it is being examined at main headquarters and he cannot share its content. She doesn't tell him they have a copy, nor does she tell him she still intends to conduct her own investigation. She's happy he doesn't ask about her detective licence and feels it means he's beginning to accept her.

After hanging up she has to justify to Norman why she didn't tell Harvey they also had the list, insisting they're within their rights to conduct a "parallel investigation." As the food arrives, Norman agrees to the deception (a word Casey objects to) but only after she promises that if they manage to identify an actual suspect from the list - he's trying to be positive about their chances - they will tell Harvey who that suspect is.

"These burgers are pretty good," Riley puts an end to discussion about the list. "But not as good as the ones at Kipp's Burgers. Kipp kills his own cattle out in back."

"Charming," Casey says. "You have to love small-town life. Beautiful scenery and local restaurateurs slaughtering cattle in the downtown core."

"Riley exaggerates. Sometimes the fish on the menu have been caught by Kipp, but I doubt he butchers cattle out back. I expect there's a by-law against that."

"I envy you guys. Growing up in a close-knit community, in a loving family. All those wide-open spaces. It's special. You're lucky."

"We are but of course Still Waters isn't perfect. We have conflict and town council meetings have been known to get a little raucous. That's always fun to cover." Norman finds opening up is feeling good, distracting him from the fear. "There's exciting things to report on now and again. Like when the uber-environmentalists staged protests over the removal of a few trees for an artificial turf field. There were pitched debates in the school parking lot and plenty of colorful quotes."

"Ah-ha. So you and your parents do report on more contentious stories than putting up a fruit stand next to the General Store."

"Yeah, sure. But it's all kept to a certain acceptable level of contention and people remain friends, or most do. In Still Waters going for a quart of milk can take forever. I've spent hours talking outside the General Store. I might have said chewing the fat, but the anti-cliché monster here would call me on it."

"Got that right," his brother says.

"So, what are you parents like?" Casey asks.

"Our Dad is neurotic," Riley says. "And our Mom is more neurotic. And our sister is even more neurotic. But they're funny about it. Our parents do stuff with us and they're great. Oh, and unlike Norman, they laugh."

"What? Is this 'dump on your big brother' day or something? Come on, I laugh. I can be funny, too."

"Yeah, right."

"I take my responsibilities seriously, that's all. But I say amusing things. Like, for example: 'watch it, Riley, or I'll club you one.'"

"Has he ever actually clubbed you one?"

"Nah." Riley stands and asks where the washroom is. Casey says, "That way, then left." Riley goes off.

It's quiet a moment.

"My parents aren't funny." Casey blurts out. Her need to share is strong and this time no voice inside her head warns her to keep away from personal details. "I mean they take life serious, always do the right thing, only sometimes the right thing isn't the right thing. Like they thought I should learn Mandarin so they put me in a class. Not fun; there are 50,000 written characters, though we only studied about 20,000 of them."

"I can do twenty-eight, tops."

"They were forever taking me to meetings with other girls adopted from China. Celebrating Chinese holidays. Eating Chinese food. The real stuff, too. Yuck."

Norman says, "Wow, what horrible parents. Trying to do what was best for you."

"You try fried pigeon. I love cheese but my Mom stopped buying it. She read the Chinese consider cheese unsavory. Only nomadic tribes ate cheese in East Asia. I finally told her to look upon me as a nomad and we went back to cheese. I did like being allowed dessert before the main course though. Still do."

"Seems like they thought a connection to your birth country would be good for you."

"I get that but it was heavy-handed."

"I expect you made friends at those meetings."

"Yeah. Brianna's great; we still hang out. Obviously I had a lot in common with all of them. Okay, you got me, I liked the meetings. But Chinese culture didn't, whatever, didn't do much for me. Thank God they let me drop the language classes. I preferred French and Je peux parler en francais tres bien. I wanted to be a Canadian, not a hyphenized Canadian."

"Fair enough."

She hesitates, but on she goes. "My parents may have wanted what was best for me but they lacked warmth somehow. I played grass hockey and when the last whistle went my father would methodically trudge off, his gumboots clumping on the ground. His Dad job done for the day he'd go back to his workshop and wine, saying little if anything about the game or how

I'd played. My mother, she didn't do hugs. Or not spontaneously. Spontaneity was not encouraged in our house. She'd give a stiff hug when she gave me a gift or when I returned from a trip with the basketball team. They were perfunctory. You know? So maybe it isn't so bad they decamped to Nova Scotia."

Norman says, "Oh I don't believe that. You may not miss them yet but you will."

Casey is enjoying this. Beats sitting across the street looking out her window at the phone booth in front of the diner. She has a thought about maintaining an air of detachment with a client but almost immediately it slips her mind.

Norman says, "You know what? I think it's great your father went to your games. And if your mother was uncomfortable hugging, the fact she hugged you at all, that has to mean something."

"Yeah. Okay. I guess. I mean I never thought of it like that," Casey really hadn't thought of it like that. She's somehow pleased that he did though. "Sure. They tried. They got out of their comfort zones for me I guess."

Norman still has a nagging feeling of futility, a feeling their efforts to find Keeley won't amount to anything and coming to the city to find the list will prove a waste of time. But somehow Casey is helping him to feel there's a chance.

He takes a leap into being even more supportive: "I'm sorry things were like that for you. You're a warm person despite that. I mean you came out of it looking pretty darn good. So to speak. Like I don't mean how you look, you know, physically. Though you do look nice."

"I look only nice?" She makes a sour face.

"Okay, no, I mean you look great; you look really, really great, in fact totally great. I better stop now."

Riley is back, he sits.

Norman looks to Casey. Now he's feeling this is a waste of time. He might sort like her and everything but they're not gonna find Keeley in a restuarant and she's not really a detective.

And the list is a bust.

"Anyhow," he says. "That list is lengthy and I don't what to do with it. But Riley and I, we should get back to Still Waters. If Keeley is released that's where we need to be."

Casey is about to ask if that means she's not invited when she notices something at the front of the diner. Peering in the diner's front window is Philip, his face scrunched up against the glass.

"Here comes trouble," she says.

A drunken Philip bursts in with a golf club tucked into his belt as if it were a sword. He seeks Norman, whom he's now fixated upon. He squints and spots the three and, pulling out his golf club with a flourish and waving it about like Rob Roy about to lead men into battle, he moves toward their table.

"There you are," he bellows at Norman. "On guard, you blackguard." Philip swings his club/sword down upon the table – SMASH! It breaks plates and mugs and spills food and drinks. "Refill anyone?" he asks.

The restaurant comes alive, some customers jump up from their seats, others cower in theirs. Philip turns to the room. "Relax people, back to your meals. I only have issue with the gentleman in the wrinkled suit. Thanks for your understanding and do have a great day."

Lindsay and one of her wait staff rush over to confront Philip, but Casey stands and holds up her hands.

"It's okay, Lindz," she says. "He's from England. I can handle him." Lindsay nods, she knows Philip well enough and knows

Casey better.

"He's of a type that responds best to rough treatment," Casey tells Norman. "So here we go."

She grabs Philip by the back of his shirt and the seat of his pants, wrenching him to the front of her table. "You are pathetic," she says, yanking him back for momentum then hurling him forward onto the table. He slides until his head hits the jukebox with a thunk. On pops Freddy Fender's 'Wasted Days and Wasted Nights.'

Norman, horrified by the violence, stands and brushes shards of broken cups from his lap. He grabs Riley, pulling him up from the table, Riley protests but Norman leads him to the exit and they are out the door.

Casey is hurt by their sudden departure. As Lindsay and her staff start picking up things from the floor, Casey just stares at the front door. Finally she turns to Philip, still prone upon the table.

"So, Philip," she says. "Are you okay? Nothing broken?"

"Not so far as I can tell."

"That's too bad. Now the important question: is your car back from the garage?"

"It is, yes, and unlike me it works fine," he says. "Even vacuumed it, front and back."

"I don't need those details. I just need the car."

Philip gets up from the table and takes a seat, rubbing his head. "That was fun." He pulls his keys out of his pocket. "It's down a block near Howe Street." He hands over the keys. "I lost my phone so can't keep in touch. Say, wonder if I might come along?"

"You most certainly might not," she says. "Thanks for the car." She heads for the door.

"I think I could use a coffee please, Lindsay."

"I think you could, too."

"Oh, and I shall pay for any damage."

"That would be nice. One coffee coming up."

"Best make it strong."

19.

Benjie has been sweating for hours in a hot car with nothing to do. Since his attempts in the morning he hasn't tried much in the way of conversation with Jerry. Peering inside cars to spot the brothers is dull and hard work and it seems improbable it will lead to anything. The cars are zooming by and Benjie is certain he would not be able to recognize them in any case.

That is *if* the brothers were to pass by, the chances of that happening seeming to Benjie to be remote in the extreme, though he wasn't going to broach that subject with Jerry again.

He is watching the younger Broom bang his gun on his hip. Hold on, something even more exciting to watch now, Jerry is no longer banging his gun on his hip but has turned to tightening the bandage on his left hand. Makes for riveting drama.

"Must be a deep cut," Benjie says. "How'd it happen?"

"Dog."

"A dog?"

"Yup."

"Care to elaborate?"

Jerry looks at Benjie. He doesn't like being questioned and is unsure of the meaning of the word elaborate. Staring at Benjie, he thinks it over and guesses that Earl's wimpy brown kid wants to know more about the dog bite and the word elaborate is a way of asking. "My dad has a dog," he finally says.

"Right. The little one. I've seen it."

"Well, it hates my guts."

"Hate's a strong word, Jerry."

"Oh it hates me all right."

"That must be painful."

"It mostly only hurt when he bit me."

"No, I meant emotional pain. You seem impervious to physical pain. I meant the dog hating you must be painful. It's your father's dog and you love your father so I thought it might be painful for you to have his dog hate your guts, as you so eloquently put it."

"No. I hate the dog as much as it hates me."

"I see. Say. Here's a question: I was thinking about my father and how I have to obey him, which I do, I do as he says, as you know. I don't always want to though. You know what I mean? So: ever say no to your father?"

"No."

"So then no matter what he tells you to do, you're okay with doing it?"

"Yes."

"Remember that Nietzsche theory I told you about? Where he suggests that we do the same thing over and over again for eternity?"

"I didn't get what you meant by that."

"Well I don't think he means we repeat what we do literally. I think he meant we should live each day as if we *had to* repeat what we do for eternity. Make that day as good as you can, even as honorable as you can."

"Yeah. So what?"

"My point is that if we keep following our fathers' orders and they keep telling us to do lousy things, wrong things, the question becomes: are we happy living like that over and over again? So: what do you think?"

"I think I'm happy doing what I do and I think that unless you wanna end up in cement like Mister Clement you better just keep watching out for them two brothers." Jerry places his finger around the trigger of his gun. "Because I am watching you."

Benjie watches cars.

20.

On the streets of downtown Vancouver, Casey has caught up to Norman and Riley and the three now approach Philip's two-door 1980s Honda Civic, rust-red, covered in dents and scratches and with a bumper sticker that reads: 'I Used To Be Cool."

"Here's Philip's car," Casey tells the brothers. There's a ticket on the front, Philip has overparked yet again, and she pulls it from under the windshield wiper, opens the passenger door, leans over and puts it in the glove box with the others.

"Who wants the front?" she calls out.

Unhappy about Casey's public battle with Philip and dealing with an extra painful burst of worry for his sister, Norman doesn't stop walking at the car but keeps going right on down the street.

"Riley, come on," is all he says.

"Hey wait," Casey says, closing the passenger door and hustling back to the sidewalk. "Where are you going?" Dodging pedestrians, she catches up to Norman, taps him on the shoulder. "What's up?" He stops. People pass, it's a busy area and she drags him over to the front of a music store where they stand next to a window display of bass guitars.

"What'd I do to deserve the cold shoulder?"

"That was a lousy display back there."

Riley says, "No it wasn't. It was awesome."

"Riley, please." Norman looks at Casey. "That kind of violent confrontation is not something I want Riley to witness."

"That wasn't so violent, was it?"

"You threw him onto the table and into a wall."

"You mean a jukebox."

"Whichever."

"Yes, well he's fine. A certain sub-set of British males have thick skulls and Philip is a member."

"That's not funny but it is culturally insensitive and weirdly untrue."

"Okay. Whatever. Sorry."

"Thank you for your help but Riley and I will be getting the bus home now."

"That's it? You go and I stay?"

"Yes. But you were helpful. Like I said before that list is long and it seems confusing and I'm not sure what's to be done with it but we should get back to our yard."

"That's your plan?"

"Yes. You can email me your invoice. And again, thanks and nice meeting you. Or mostly nice. Partially. Right, well, we better get going; I'll let you know when we find her." He once more starts up walking.

"You'll let me know?"

"Riley, come on."

She follows. "There has to be something else going on here besides Philip's nonsense and a remark about Brits. Wait. Did we share too much? Is that it?"

"Don't be ridiculous. Keep up Riley, please."

"Hey. Norman," Casey is up beside him. "News flash: you can't just write about life. You do know that, right?" He walks fast but she keeps keeping up. "You have to take part in it. To *do* things. Even when it gets messy." She's loud, people look. "That is what being in the world requires." She grabs his shoulder and turns him to look at her. "That you deal with shit. You take risks."

"Not Norman," Riley says. "He just goes to work."

Norman has had enough and holds his right hand in front of his face, his palm out, silencing them. He goes to speak but is too angry; purses his lips, waits a moment, puts his hand down, tries again. "That is crap," he manages under his breath. He points an index finger at Casey. "I am all about action." He turns to his brother and now points at him. "By the way, Riley, going to work *is* action. Among other things, it puts food on the table and serves our community. And don't you even mention the word cliche." He finally puts his finger down; he turns back to Casey. "Being a man of action, however, does not mean I have to condone violence or the making of a display of oneself in public. That is not something life requires of me or anyone. Now get moving, Riley, we're going."

Norman resumes walking.

"Nice speech," Casey says, darting after him. "But hey what happened back there wasn't entirely my fault. I try to help Philip and he doesn't always behave himself. But he's my neighbour. A friend. We nearly had a fling. Okay, we did but it wasn't a quality fling."

"I don't need to know that, thank you," Norman says.

"He's lonely and fooled himself into thinking he's in love with me so he sees you as his rival. It's a twisted jealousy based on the fact that most days he lives in an alcoholic fog. I mean it has no basis in fact. You and I aren't in a relationship. Clearly. I mean I don't even like you in any particularly meaningful way. Not to be rude but I find you an irritating, stuffy and morally superior person." She pauses. "Why did I just say that?" She seeks a way to change the subject but stutters. Finally, she just says that Philip is harmless, adding that "admittedly he is not mentally sound."

"Yeah, he's from England," Riley says.

Norman stops. "Riley, let us not make assumptions about an entire country based upon one person. You're only mimicking her anyways."

Riley says, "Mimicking's a cool word. Where'd you read that?"

Norman looks to Casey. "Look, you can be a free spirit but please don't teach my brother prejudices and I'm sorry but we need to go home so once again: thank you for your help and goodbye." He is off, walking faster this time, bumps into a man in a suit, says nothing, the man frowns, Norman keeps going.

Casey and Riley scramble after him.

"Okay," Casey says. "Sorry. I shouldn't talk like that in front of your brother or at all. And people from England shouldn't be thrown into jukeboxes; after all they make great fish and chips - I've been there so I know - and I cheer for their soccer team every World Cup. So please just let me drive you back to Still Waters. No more public scenes and nothing personal will pass my lips. Which I'm not saying has anything to do with this but I know you're a little timid that way, like emotionally, or whatever, and I respect that."

"He's not timid," Riley says. "He's a flat-out fraidy-cat."

"Would you two stop?" Norman turns and walks back, speaking sotto voce. "I am neither timid nor afraid; or any other pejorative label denoting cowardice. What I am is *going home*. On the bus. And you Riley are coming with me." He turns, moving even more quickly, he's dodging people like a halfback avoiding tackles.

Again, Casey and Riley bolt after him.

"Hey, wait. You can't go back, not right away." Casey pulls out her phone. "Not on the bus you can't. Hold on."

She's too busy being in the moment to know why she's conducting herself with such a large dollop of desperation, though the thought crosses her mind that finishing the job is mandatory. Or is the real reason not just wanting to help Norman but to be around him? Re-focusing on the job at hand, she madly punches in letters on her phone as she struggles to keep up with Norman.

"Okay," she says. "Got it. Thought this might be the case. Look at this: the next bus for Still Waters doesn't leave for five hours. See for yourself." She holds out her phone.

He stops but doesn't look.

Riley does. "Yup. Five hours. Five-and-a-half hours. You wanna hang around the city for five-and-a-half hours with nothing to do but bump into people?"

Casey says, "And then ride home with whatever idiots might be on that bus?"

"Yeah," Riley says. "Did you see the guy who was picking his nose?"

Casey says, "Totally gross!"

Norman did see the guy and it *was* gross. Not the kind of person he's accustomed to sharing confined spaces with. He realizes he does not share confined spaces well, period, not with anyone. A car is a confined space but at least he won't be sharing it with strangers. He next wonders if that thought represents a tacit approval of Casey. *She's not a stranger anymore?*

He turns to her. "Okay," he says at last. "We'll go in the car. But this doesn't mean you're hired."

"Understood."

117

"It also doesn't mean I approve of your methods."

"I've crossed boundaries, I get that."

"It just means I'm accepting a ride to my yard, with gratitude, so I can get on with the job of finding my sister. That's what's important here."

"Obviously and absolutely," Casey says. "And we will find her. So let's get started."

Norman notes Casey included herself again, using the pronoun 'we' as if he'd hired her. He doesn't approve of that but lets it go.

They walk back to Philip's car and find another ticket on the windshield. Casey tells them it doesn't matter, Philip never pays them anyhow. Riley claims the front seat, which is fine with Norman, who squeezes into the back and immediately has trouble with the seat-belt. He's not going to tell his brother and be mocked for it so he continues trying to fit the two ends together.

"This car is so old you wind the windows down *manually*," Riley notes. "Like with your hands. Sick, hey?"

"Aren't they all like that?" Norman asks.

Riley says, "Hey, Casey, we got a Hutterite in back."

Casey is about to turn the ignition when she notices two elderly women across the street who seem to be filming them. She squints. They look familiar. "Be right back." Out she gets.

Traffic is heavy so she holds up her hand and stops the car on her left; as she steps toward the other lane, she adroitly waves a truck on before holding up her other hand and getting the next vehicle to stop; she now deftly scoots to the other side.

"I will give her this," Norman says. "She's pretty good at crossing streets."

Gaining the sidewalk, Casey walks over to the two women. "Hi. My name is Casey Collier. Sorry to bother you but I was wondering…weren't you at the Miller yard last night? In Still Waters? Then this morning you were in the window across the street, right?"

"We were also on the bus," Agnes says.

"I'm Margaret, this is Agnes. We're the Millers neighbours and I imagine you're curious about what we're doing here."

"I am; I was wondering about the camera."

"Well we're both past 75 and have lived in Still Waters most of our lives," Margaret begins. "Agnes was a grade below me in school. She is a member of the Ktunaxa Nation of the interior and a retired teacher. I am Scottish and Welsh and I was an accountant. We are together. A couple."

Agnes says, "We're legally married."

"Congratulations."

"We were there when James, Lana and Norman moved across the street in their motor home; Norman was two." Agnes says. "We're godmothers to Riley and Keeley and babysat all three. They're wonderful children."

"That's sweet," Casey says. "But so why are you – "

"Filming them?" Margaret asks. Casey nods. "I shall explain: James and Lana asked us to keep an eye on their children. They were nervous about leaving them alone for the first time. Our plan was to make a movie to show how well things went while they were away. We didn't expect things to go sideways."

Agnes says, "We wish we'd been home last night. We could have alerted Harvey."

"We do not intend to miss any more action."

"We were hoping you came here to pick Keeley up," Agnes says.

"No, afraid not and there's been no ransom demand," Casey tells them. "But we have a lead and we're going back to Still Waters. It's not a big car but I'm sure we could fit you in the back somehow."

"Oh that's all right." Margaret says. "We don't want to become part of the story. That's not something journalists do and we feel we're following a story now."

"The Millers taught us well," Agnes smiles. "We write for the paper now and again and have put video stories up on the website. Oh. Here. For your drive back or later on." Agnes pulls out a bag from her backpack and gives it to Casey. She tells her it's a fresh supply of her home-made bannock.

Casey marvels to herself about what a wonderful thing it must be to have neighbours who offer help and become babysitters and godparents, who make movies and give you food. She gives them a warm good-bye.

Margaret films Casey as she crosses the street, stepping aside for a cyclist, waving a bus through, her road crossing skills very much on display.

"Well?" Norman asks as she gets back in. "What did Agnes and Margaret say?"

"Your parents asked them to keep an eye on you guys so they're making a movie or something. Oh, they gave us this," she passes the bag back to Norman. "It's called bannock I believe."

"You don't know bannock hey?" Norman says. "It's a flat bread. I have enjoyed Agnes' bannock all my life." He puts it on the seat and resumes struggling with his belt. "Okay, I'm not sure my seat-belt works."

Riley reaches back and snaps his brother's seat-belt in, he'd been trying to fit it in the wrong clip.

As Casey puts the Honda in gear, Riley pulls himself out his open window and raises his head over the roof to wave in the direction of Agnes and Margaret's camera.

"Hi Mom, hi Dad. Having a wonderful time only Norman is a wimp!" He ducks back in.

"When this is over, Riley, remind me to club you one."

21.

Casey only gets a block before realizing she needs a change of clothing and her phone charger and doubles back to her apartment. She suggests Norman might enjoy people watching from his vantage point in the back seat of Philip's car, and that Riley might enjoy teasing Norman while he does, and that is exactly what they do. Norman unrolls his window and gawks at Vancouverites rushing by while Riley makes smart-ass comments about the people and about Norman experiencing the big city for the first time.

Casey goes inside alone and as she steps off the elevator on her floor her phone rings. It's her parents from Nova Scotia; she doesn't answer. Once in the door a text arrives that reads: *We miss you please call.* She stares at it a long time, so long she forgets what she came to her apartment to do.

Forgetting about her charger, all she remembers is that she needs to change. After all, she slept on a park bench and could use a shower, too. She takes a quick one. She puts on a clean pair of black yoga pants and grabs a light green t-shirt. Same loafers. Stuffs a night shirt and toiletries into a small shoulder bag. You never know, she thinks, might have to stay in Still Waters again.

She wants to.

They make their way out of the city and Casey proves to be as artful a driver as she is a crosser-of-streets. Agnes and Margaret rented a budget friendly gold-coloured Pontiac Sunfire and when they merged onto the Trans-Canada they were only a mile in back of the Honda.

Meanwhile, Benjie and Jerry sit in the same black car in the same blazing sun watching the same section of highway with the same odds of recognizing faces they don't know fly by in an unknown vehicle. Jerry is of course still determined to kidnap the brothers while Benjie continues to be conflicted. On the one hand he feels an obligation to his father and the promise he made his mother, on the other he feels guilty about the little girl in her room in the woods, alone and scared.

By taking the Trans-Canada, the fastest route, Casey, doing well over 100 kilometres an hour, will pass the intersection where the Cadillac sits. About a mile from it, Riley asks Norman if he is enjoying his first car ride. Norman testily reminds Riley that he has been in a car before but says he can't remember going this fast. Talking slowly, Norman's face looks as if he just stuffed a dozen scorching hot red peppers into his mouth.

"I think I was right about Norman getting car sick," Riley says. Casey looks in her rear-view mirror. "You okay?" she asks.

"Not really," Norman slowly says. "You're going so fast. I think I might throw up actually. Yeah, I'm definitely gonna throw up."

"Oh boy." Casey quickly pulls over onto the roadside.

"Get out! Quick!" Riley yells. "It'll smell and you'll make me clean it up."

Norman stumbles out his door and takes a few steps before leaning over and puking onto the roadside. Spitting out bits of vomit, he wipes his face with the back of his hand, straightens up and promptly vomits again.

Casey pulled over directly across from Jerry Broom and Benjie Porter and the two watch a man throw up onto the roadside. Benjie, grossed out, looks away but Jerry stares. There's something about that guy. He grabs the photos of the Miller brothers, looking from the picture of the older brother to the man and back again.

"Benjie. It's him! Look at this!" He shoves the photo over to Benjie. "That guy there is Norman Miller. Look!" Benjie looks and nods, as hard as it is to believe, it does look like the puking guy is the same guy in the photo. "This is a miracle," Jerry says, "My father is right: God does work in mysterious ways."

Across the highway, Norman lurches back to the Honda and climbs in the back seat; Casey looks in her rear-view and asks if he's okay and he nods.

She pulls back into traffic.

"Got 'cha," Jerry mutters, turning the key in the ignition and sticking his gun out the window. "Here we go. Try and knock out a tire."

"You're not serious, are you?" Benjie replies. Jerry fires his gun out the window. "You are serious."

Casey is back on the highway. "Was that a car backfiring? she asks. "There it goes again."

Riley sees a Cadillac turn onto the highway, forcing a golden Pontiac Sunfire to brake hard; now the Cadillac is in behind the Honda.

Riley shouts, "A black Cadillac!" Another gunshot. "Hey those arent't backfires, they're shooting at us!"

"Down!" Casey shouts. Riley and Norman duck and she scrunches low. A shot shatters a brake light.

In the Cadillac, Jerry drives with his gun out the window. "I could use some help so you better pull your trigger or you're gonna end up –"

"I know: in cement like Mister Clement." Benjie has never fired a gun but reluctantly takes his out. He examines it and Jerry looks over to see him attempting to pull the hammer back.

"That's a double-action revolver which means you don't hafta pull the hammer back," Jerry says. "You can just fire it. So point it at a tire and pull the trigger. Do it!"

Benjie sticks his gun out and when Jerry goes back to driving, fires twice, but off into the woods.

"Just missed," he says.

After Agnes and Margaret were cut-off in their Pontiac Sunfire they soon realized the Cadillac was after the Honda and became determined to keep up. Margaret floors it past 120 kilometres, their rental trying to catch up to the Cadillac.

The Honda is rattling so bad Casey worries it might come apart and she decides desperate times call for desperate measures, and says so out loud.

"Cliché," Riley says. "Massive one."

"Hang on." Casey's veers into the other lane and is now driving right at a large oil truck.

"Is this smart?" Riley asks.

"We'll find out."

The truck honks. There's not much shoulder and if the driver of the truck cranks it to the right he'll slide down an embankment. Either he has to veer into the lane Casey just vacated or she has to steer back into it; she ignores his blaring horn and keeps barrelling at him.

Norman and Riley scream.

At the last moment the truck swerves into the other lane, only barely missing the Honda and now heading directly at the Cadillac.

Benjie holds his hands over his eyes and he screams as Jerry cranks his wheel to the right and the Cadillac flies off the highway, bumping violently down an embankment until hitting a fir tree – THUD!

On the highway, the truck steers back into its rightful lane, avoiding a gold Pontiac Sunfire.

Agnes and Margaret's first inclination is to stop and see if the men in the Cadillac are okay but having seen them shoot at the Honda they decide it best to keep driving.

Casey is back in her lane continuing on to Still Waters. "Is it just me," she says. "Or was that too close for comfort." Riley doesn't bother pointing out the cliche.

Down the embankment, Jerry tries to restart the car while Benjie works to open the damaged passenger door. After a few tries, the Caddy starts and Jerry reverses away from the tree and with a series of turns and backing-ups coaxes the big car back up the slope. He makes it to the side of the highway and stops, gets out and checks the front-end; the right front tire is deflated. He leans into the Cadillac. "Cops might show up; we need to get out of here fast," he tells Benjie. "So put some air in that front tire and let's go."

"Will do," Benjie says. "Soon as I can get my door open."

22.

It is evening, shortly after dark, and a warm, gentle breeze blows through the Miller family's homeless yard. It's the kind of summer weather that a mere two days ago would have seen Riley outside with friends playing baseball, catching fish at the local lagoon, teasing girls they crossed paths with and getting teased back. After dinner they might have played more sports or video games and by now they'd be half-way through a movie, their obsession of late being films based upon Stephen King novels.

Instead, Riley spent his day in the big city looking for clues to the disappearance of his sister and was a passenger in a car shot at by men with real guns. And now he is in his yard quietly counting the number of owners of black Cadillacs on a lengthy list he illegally obtained from the motor vehicle branch. He's also eating a carrot slice, which Norman insisted he wrap up in a napkin and take after Riley left it on his plate at a local restaurant; carrots are good for your eyes, his brother told him. "And that is not a cliché but a nutritional fact."

Norman is not with his brother just now. He left the restuarant early to go to the newspaper office to write a story about the local Fish and Wildlife club and check the proofs to see Jack has the next edition laid-out for press. He did this because it was necessary and because he needed something to take his mind off the constant worry about his sister.

Here's this: not only did he not tell Casey to return to Vancouver, he asked her to keep an eye on Riley while he was at the office, making her promise she would keep him within ten feet of her at all times.

So Casey is in the yard with Riley, sitting against a tree a few feet behind him. Norman trusting her to keep an eye on him pleased her, even though he couldn't leave it at that and added that watching Riley didn't mean she was hired as the family detective.

She is enjoying being in a neighbourhood quieter than hers, one with a view of the sky not impeded by buildings. Staring up at the stars she again has the thought that a small town would suit her fine.

This small town would, in fact.

Half-an-hour ago her parents called and, as before, she did not answer. This time they left a voice mail, which she checked; her mother said they were worried and asked her to call. Thinking of family gets her thinking of what it might have been like to have a bigger and more loving one. Then a small thought knocks on the door of her emotional world and she lets it in: *In their own way they are loving.*

She watches Riley counting Caddy owners. She finds him both a thorough counter and, moving his lips quietly as he adds, an amusing one. He's a terrific kid. "I know I told you this already but you're a pretty cool guy, Riley," she tells him.

He holds up his hand to concentrate as he finishes and feels for a pen he'd put down on the ground . "Thanks," he says to Casey. "Tell it to my brother."

"I think he knows already."

Finding the pen, Riley writes the number down. "Who would have thought there'd be 329 owners of black Cadillacs in B.C.?"

"Lemme see." Riley passes her the list. "The one we're looking for is probably registered in Vancouver. Which I see most of them are."

"Yeah," Riley says. "Vancouver and Victoria. I was dumb and forgot to look for the licence plate number when they were chasing us. That would have been good."

"You need to cut yourself some slack, Riley. We were being shot at. You know, guns. Anyhow, I looked and there was tape over it."

"Nice. Performance under pressure. You're a good driver, too. Like really good."

"Thanks. That Honda's a manual shift. Extra fun."

"You're kinda like the Letterkenny guys."

"Okay. Sweet. Only who are the Letterkenny guys?"

"These guys on TV that live in a town called Letterkenny, in Ontario. Wayne and Daryl. When they get an idea they do it, even if it's a dumb one; like you do. Like they thought of setting up this fart-sharing website and then they just went right ahead and did it. Just like that. Actually, that idea was a pretty good one."

"I appreciate the comparison."

"My boring brother thinks Wayne and Daryl are annoying and weird."

"Well dissing Wayne and Daryl might show bad judgment on your brother's part but I'd still say he has a few good qualities."

"Like which ones?"

"Like keeping his nose to the grindstone."

"Cliché."

"How about watching out for you guys and caring for you. He loves you and he'd do anything in the world for you. And don't tell me that's a cliché because if it is then it's one we could all use a lot more of."

"I guess. It's kinda soapy though."

She has him talking about real things and he's taking her seriously. "Do you miss your sister?"

"I guess I do." Riley is quiet a moment, he's really giving it some thought. "I mean like if she was on a vacation or something and I knew she was all right I wouldn't miss for a while but eventually I might. But I don't know she's all right so, yeah, even though it's only been one day, I kinda do miss her. I miss her a lot actually."

"We will find her and I look forward to actually seeing her this time. I also look forward to meeting your parents. Hey, here comes Sparky." Riley loves that impromptu nickname for his brother.

"Good one," he says, leaning back and reaching out to give Casey a fist bump.

Norman walks into the yard. "You brush your teeth?" he asks Riley.

"No bathroom. You know bathrooms, the place where tooth-brushes are kept?"

"He ate his carrot slice, Norman. Carrots are good for both the eyes and the teeth." She winks at Riley and he gives her another fist bump.

Norman tells him it's time to bed down. "Take a moment to make sure the ground you pick isn't lumpy or you'll wake up with a sore back. Try bundling up that badminton net for a pillow. And in case the bad guys show up pick a spot where you'll be hard to find."

"That's too many instructions," Riley says. "And you're being paranoid."

"Being paranoid doesn't have to mean being wrong. After all, it's the law of averages, some paranoid people have gotta be right."

Riley does his eye roll thing and moves off to find a place to sleep at the back of the yard.

Norman sits near Casey. "I didn't think to get the licence while we were being shot at." he says. "Harvey spoke to Agnes and Margaret, they didn't get it either. He said they didn't get a look at whoever was shooting at us."

"So everyone's worried about the licence plate. Well I looked in my rear-view. You didn't miss anything. It was taped over."

"Nice job."

"I already got some love from your brother about that. What else did Harvey say?"

"They ran the Cadillac owner names through their data base but no one with a serious criminal record came back. They're checking out a few though."

"If they checked under your real name, the one starting with an 'h', bet they'd find someone with a connection to your family. Be nice to know what that name is. You know of family or past friends that might know it?"

"I do not. Grandparents dead. Father no siblings, my mother's sister lives in England; I don't even know where. And I remain skeptical about this different name thing. You haven't said who told you that."

"It's just what I heard."

"Sometimes you sound believable. This isn't one of those times."

"Sorry, best I can do."

"Is there any bannock left?"

"Oh, it was good. And yeah, we left you some."

She tosses him the bag and he takes out the last of the bannock and starts munching. "Harvey suggested we stay somewhere else; I declined."

"Yeah, well security is definitely a concern now."

"His night guy is gonna spend his shift parked down the road. It seems like an overreaction but then I can't figure why someone would steal our motor home and take shots at us. But there has to be a connection."

"If it was just a bunch of thieves then why try and kill you? If they even *were* trying to kill you. I got the impression they were aiming for the tires. Maybe they were trying to kidnap you guys. You sure you haven't written a story someone didn't like."

"Oh I'm sure I have written a story someone didn't like. But not so as they'd kidnap Keeley to get revenge. We don't get that serious in this town."

"Okay, so then are you sure your parents haven't kept something from you?"

"Yeah, I am. Pretty much. You know, even if someone is after us, which is really unlikely, I'm not gonna be chased out of my own home. Or my own yard."

Riley calls out, "Atta boy, Norman!"

"Go to sleep!"

"How did the story go?" Casey asks. She's genuinely interested and it keeps him talking and keeps her learning about the family.

"It got done. Fish and Wildlife work with stream keepers to keep creeks and streams free of debris. It's mostly old people putting on galoshes and wading into water. I like them and they do a lot of good."

"Is it boring writing about stuff like that?"

"My parents gave me the community environment beat when I was Riley's age, so it's routine. But I respect what volunteers do and want people to know about it."

"I bet you're a great writer."

"I work hard at it. Stick to basics with news stories. Lighter news and profiles, that's where I have fun. I wrote a story about our co-ed 7-aside soccer league while I was playing in a game. I didn't play great but I got a good story. I use a lot of quotes and my subjects don't have to be an official or a cop or own a business. I do profiles on anyone, including kids and pets. In a small community a newspaper should be about people and their lives, not just about what passes for news."

"So then is the latest paper ready to roll, or whatever you call it?"

IIe nods. "It's ready to go to press, yes. I'm afraid Jack buried your pumpkin story on page twelve. Looks good though."

"So...did you read it?"

"Of course. The alliteration was a little strong in your lead. 'Piers Mahortoff has produced a positively perfect and prodigious pumpkin.'"

"Alliteration is bad?"

"It was fine. Something different wakes our readers up. You have a natural instinct for narrative. You read much?"

"Sure. Mystery novels mostly."

"Try the new journalists. Chuck Palahniuk, Joan Didion, Gay Talese. Insightful writers who work the language well and get beyond the tried and true. They write about people and culture."

"I'll keep it in mind," she tells him. "After all, I can't stick with 'M is for Malice' forever."

"Sue Grafton, right?"

"The alphabet series. I like detective stories."

"No surprise there."

"Agatha Christie, Sir Arthur Conan Doyle. Dashiell Hammett; when I was a little girl I wanted to marry Nick Charles."

"Those are good writers; I expect you've learnt a lot about writing without knowing it. Anyhow, I hardly changed a word in your story. It was good."

She's more than a bit chuffed about the compliment. "Really?" she says. "I mean you're not just saying it was good to be nice?"

"No. You used the right information and ordered it well and it was clear and had a nice flow."

"Okay. Thanks. By the way, thanks for letting me stay. I hope to return the favor one day. Norman Miller sleeping in the big city. Stranger things have happened."

Riley calls out from the back of the yard: "No way!"

"Goodnight, Riley!" Norman yells.

It's quiet a moment. Casey is thinking of how pushy she was earlier and is trying to decide if she should apologize. In the end she figures it won't do any harm.

"Hey," she says. "I'm sorry about those questions I threw at you today. I don't feel too good about that."

"You mean about my life without buses and cars?"

"I was pretty nosey."

"For the record I don't like buses and cars so I avoid them. I grew up sheltered and that probably has something to do with why I feel that way and why I love routine and stay close to home. Kids are supposed to be given a chance to fail. I never had that."

Casey tells herself to shut right up. He's talking. Letting his guard down. She nods attentively and tries her best to exude a measure of sympathy.

134

"They never let me out of their sight," Norman is saying. "I couldn't walk ten feet in front of them without being scooped up. They'd stand on either side of me like they were guarding a key witness in a mafia murder trial."

"Why were they like that?"

"I don't know. Their nature? Maybe they were outliers, I mean to some degree aren't all parents overprotective of their first born?"

"So I've heard. Mine weren't so much. At least my Chinese parents weren't. Ha ha."

"Oh. Yeah."

"Sorry, bad joke."

"Actually, it was kinda funny. Anyhow all I know is that by the time Riley came along things changed; two of us, then three, put constrains on their time and they relaxed a bit. It was too late for me to be normal though."

She makes a face she intends to be skeptical and supportive both; it mostly just comes off as scrunched up. "Oh, come on, I'd say your normal. Or no more non-normal than anyone else. Or only a little non-normal."

"Thanks."

"You ever consider they gave you more space because over time they became less afraid of the past?" Before Norman can comment, Casey's phone beeps. She hits mute. "Philip. Best to ignore. Oh, my parents called."

"That's nice. Did you talk for long?"

"Twice they called. I didn't answer either time but they sent a text. Said they'd send a plane ticket if I'd visit. My guess is they're feeling guilty."

"My guess is they want to see their daughter and I hope you take them up on their offer."

"I might. I mean maybe. I mean like, you know, down the road."

Norman doesn't exactly dislike all this opening up and sharing but it is definitely tiring and he's definitely tired. He catches himself yawning and apologizes.

"No, I understand," Casey says. "Long and emotional day and you didn't get much sleep last night."

Norman says, "Yeah and you slept on a park bench. So I guess we should get ourselves ready for bed here. Let's stake out our...our patches of earth."

Casey is happy she won't be on that bench again and even more happy Norman has warmed up to her enough that he's okay with her staying in his yard. She watches him take a sleeping bag and find a patch of grass and then grabs the other bag and stands over a patch of grass about twelve feet from Norman's.

"Okay if I lay here?" she asks. "I won't bite."

"Sure. Wherever."

He begins to undress, awkwardly telling her not to worry as he's wearing a pair of boxer shorts. She says she wasn't expecting the underwear equivalent of a Speedo and adds that she doesn't intend to look in any case. Norman takes his pants off, folds them and places them neatly on the ground and, in boxer shorts and a t-shirt, crawls into his sleeping bag.

Secretly, Casey watched out of the corner of her eye and rather liked what she saw. Lean but firm.

Now it is Norman's turn to secretly watch her out of the corner of his eye. She had considered changing behind a tree but she's had a long relationship with being bold and decides to eschew modesty. Standing over her patch of grass, she slips off her black yoga pants and, what the heck, it's warm out, her top, too, and stands in white panties and bra. Her skin is a warm light brown and her shape nicely curved and Mister Peek-Out-From-His-Sleeping-Bag likes what he sees.

Casey takes the night shirt out of her shoulder bag and pulls it over her head and drops it on. It covers barely half the way down her ass and Norman does not fail to notice. He feels guilty for liking what he sees, not because he looked at her but because until he finds his sister he doesn't feel right about experiencing pleasure.

Casey slides into her sleeping bag and the two lie, close, but not too close, looking up at the night sky.

"These are awesome stars," she says. "The darkness of the sky here at night is really something. The stars. You forget about this in the city."

"I've always loved the night, the darker the better. I bet you find that strange for a coward."

"I did not say you were a coward. I said you were timid. There's a difference. What I really think is that Norman Miller is smart. For living here. For being a writer. For paying attention to things that matter." She smiles. "And I also think Norman Miller is smart not to bother with cars and buses. Not to mention revolving doors and elevators and -"

"Okay okay, that's enough…"

"You actually did pretty good today. I mean it."

"Let's just say I learned a lot. Were Agnes and Margaret by with their camera?"

"Not exactly. They did film from their window though. We waved."

"Did they tell you they're married?"

"They mentioned it in Vancouver, yes."

"The first LGBTQ wedding in Still Waters history; the only one. We covered it extensively. We had three letters to the editor against it and Agnes and Margaret insisted we printed them. Then Agnes went to each letter-writer's home and explained how she loved Margaret from the moment she saw her – when she was seven and Margaret eight. She told them those feelings came naturally to her. She invited them to the wedding and each one of them came. And brought gifts. I'll never forget one of those people, a character in town most of us know, going over and congratulating Agnes and then thanking her for helping him become a better person. Those two women are the worst bowlers in town, hands and feet worse than anyone, which is why they're so bad, uncoordinated hands and feet, but a week before the wedding they won the coveted town bowling title. Their teammates were an eleven-year-old Riley Miller and his sassy seven-year-old sister Keeley. In the final, the other teams kept on 'accidentally-on-purpose' missing shots; soon Agnes and Margaret figured it out and said they should stop. They didn't. When it was over the entire bowling alley started applauding and everyone hugged and wept. Riley and Keeley were pretty thrilled to have their name on the winning trophy. Lots of tears that night. Twist my arm and I might admit to shedding a few. That wedding was one of the biggest and grandest events in Still Waters history."

"That is a wonderful story," Casey says. "And this is a wonderful town and your newspaper is a big part of it."

Casey can't say anything else because she softly begins to cry into the crook of her arm. She doesn't let on though. Her tears are in part courtesy Norman's story but also because she feels the loss of a little girl she's never seen. Her tears are also the result of spending time with Norman and Riley, of being a part of something good, even in a bad time.

They are the tears of a lonely heart.

For Norman, his time with Casey has created a feeling that is angling toward trust. That's not exactly an emotion, trust, technically it is a 'feeder' of emotions, but whatever, he finds himself in a place he normally does not go, not with the girlfriends he's had, not with anyone outside of his family. A chance to open up?

"Casey?" he says, almost in a whisper. "It was nice of you to say I did okay out there, but no, I don't think I did. I did discover the dimensions of my limitations and I expect that's a start. I expect growth being thrust upon me is a good thing but truth is I don't know if I'm capable of taking care of myself, let alone my family."

"Oh you are. You may not know it yet, but you are."

It's quiet as they look up at the stars. "Keeley must be lonely," Norman finally says. "And afraid and angry, with me. I want her back. I want my parents back."

"I know. And you'll have them all back. You'll be a lucky and a rich man again."

"Yeah." He picks up his notebook and his flashlight pen. "I think I'll make some notes before sleeping."

"Do you always do that? Make notes?"

"It's what a writer does."

"So will today wind up being a story in the newspaper?"

"Might be too long and complex for the Current. Too personal. I will tell this story though, if not in the newspaper somewhere, in some other way. But frst we have to make what romance writers call an HEA, a happy ever after. I don't believe in tragedies."

"Me neither," Casey says. She wonders if she'll be in the story but thinks better of asking and closes her eyes.

Norman writes.

23.

Richard O'Farrell, the maintenance man at the newspaper who pointed out the Cadillac to Jack Smith outside the bank, hates the third hole at the Crippen Valley Golf Course. There's a dog-leg he can never get a ball around, shanks it to the left when the leg bends to the right. Still, he's among the best golfers in Still Waters and has twice won the annual Chamber of Commerce competition. His other claim to fame is being a relative of a soldier who died with General George Custer in Montana in 1876 at The Battle of the Little Bighorn, also known by the name the Plains Indians gave it, The Battle of the Greasy Grass, and, most popularly, as Custer's Last Stand. His exact name is on the plaque at the battle site honoring the army dead. Richard has been twice, as a youngster and again to show his children, who were in their teens and not impressed with the fact that someone in their distant family tree had the same name as their father and died at Custer's Last Stand, for teens in Still Waters are like teens everywhere: not impressed with their parents.

The entire town knows about his claim to fame because Richard has told everyone so his golfing buddies call the third hole 'O'Farrell's Last Stand.' On this day, early, so early that back in town Norman, Riley and Casey still lay in their sleeping bags, Richard shanks his first fairway shot too far left and it hits a tree with a resounding *thwack!*. He'd sent the ball 125 yards but it ricocheted off the tree and flew back 60 yards in the direction it came before rolling down the incline another 35 yards. That left it not so far from a frustrated Richard O'Farrell. "Damn!" he curses. "Again!" As his two golfing buddies howl, he and his 5-wood run headlong at that ball, covering the distance in a blip, and, without considering the mechanics of his swing, Richard comes up alongside it and drives it, hard. Up, up and over the trees that ball goes, disappearing into the stratosphere.

His friends laugh, and one, Tim, begins counting to three and the other, Gary, picks up on his intent and on the count of three, this is what, in perfect unison, Tim and Gary yell: "O'Farrell's Last Stand!" Richard drops his club and shakes his head. "Yeah yeah," he says.

At that precise moment, the ball Richard struck is hitting the back window of an already damaged Cadillac parked next to a motor home in a clearing 200 yards from where it began its flight. A cannonading drive through woods and glass, it comes to rest in the car's back seat. When it crashed through the window, Jerry had just finished checking to make sure he had tape for the licence in the glove box and was about to turn the ignition on; Benjie was approaching the passenger door, which he repaired enough it could once more open and close. Smash!

"What the hell was that?" Jerry barks out.

As Earl comes out of the motor home and asks what the noise was, Benjie opens the back door and finds broken glass all over the seat and the floor. There's a golf ball on the seat and he grabs it and flips it over to his father.

"Golf ball," Benjie says. "Big hole in the back window."

"Don't worry about it," Earl tells his son. "Just do your bidding."

Jerry says, "Yeah. Get in." Jerry did not sleep well, he had the brothers in his sight and he's angry with himself for letting them get away. He failed his father and is determined to make up for it. Benjie gets in, Jerry turns the key and the car, damaged from driving off the highway and over an embankment and now with a hole in the back window, drives off.

Flipping the ball in his big paw, Earl hits the switch on the generator and it hums into life. He goes back inside the motor home where the Reverend Broom is looking for jam so Earl takes it from the mini-cupboard and hands it to him.

Now he's at Keeley's door. "Hey," he calls. "What kind of cereal you want for your breakfast?" She tells him to shut-up. "Very nice. Here you go then. Eat this." He pulls up the door-slot and stuffs the golf ball through, laughing as it bounces around her room.

Reverend Broom is getting restless. He wants to get on with his revenge and leave the country for their new ministry in Guyana. He hates having budget issues and accuses Earl of paying too much for their flight. Earl patiently reminds him he booked on-line using Cheapflights and got the best deal possible. Now the Reverend complains he has been given marmalade, which, in his opinion, is not jam at all. "Marmalade is all they got," Earl tells him.

Inside her room, Keeley picks up the golf ball.

24.

Back in Still Waters, Cpl. Harvey Kwong parks his cruiser across from the Miller yard and spots three sleeping lumps in there. The one near the back he figures must be Riley, it's a smaller lump, and there are two near the front of the yard. Harvey surmises one of those two must be Casey and is surprised Norman allowed her to spend the night.

Bad news is never easy to give, during training at the RCMP headquarters in Regina they did a simulation on how best to approach it and Harvey thinks back to that day. Yeah. Get them to sit and don't stretch it out. He wonders if telling them while they're lying down is okay. It looks like it would have to do. Of course the news about Norman's parents isn't necessarily bad, it doesn't have to mean they are dead, but it does seem likely they are. Still, hope lived, however tenuously, and that should make the telling easier.

He walks to the first two bundles, about twelve feet apart, identifies Norman, leans over and gives him a little shake. "Hey, Norman." Eyes open groggily. "You manage to get much sleep?" Harvey straightens back up.

Norman's eyes slowly open and he looks up. "Harvey?" Harvey nods. "Yeah, I slept a little I guess; better than the night before." Norman had spent almost two hours writing notes about the past two days and that tired him out enough that he was able to fall asleep.

Harvey says, "I see your friend's still tagging along."

Casey is awake. "Tagging along?"

"Accompanying," Harvey says, noting the irritation in Casey's voice. "How's that?"

"Is there any news?" Casey asks, sitting up.

"There is. Okay to tell it, Norman?"

Norman nods, "Yeah."

"Afraid it's not good. It concerns your parents. We found their car submerged in Lake Still Waters. We're pulling it out now. They're not inside but we have divers looking. I'm sorry."

Norman reacts to this news much differently than he did to the news of Keeley. He lies there looking up at the sky, half-hearing, half-seeing, vaguely aware that Harvey and Casey are peering down and asking if he's okay. He sees Riley, angry, yelling, throwing hockey sticks. Norman takes it in as if he's in a dream, a nightmare, and when he closes his eyes he feels his heart thumping rapidly. His parents gone? It can't be. And now him the head of the family? Some leader. 'Why can't I move?' he thinks. 'But I can. I just have to *want* to.' He sits up.

"I wanna go to the lake."

Norman and Riley walk to the office of the Current while Casey drives Philip's Honda there. Harvey leaves to return to overseeing the car's recovery at the lake, where they all plan to meet. At the office, Norman uses the facilities and, while Riley is in there puts on coffee.

Casey arrives and waits for Riley to come out of the bathroom. She notices the latest edition of the paper and flips through it. She thinks about how her first byline in a newspaper, even though it's just a story about a large vegetable, should have been an exciting moment but with the events of the past two days it is not.

By the time they join Harvey at the lake the Miller sedan is nearly ready to be pulled to shore by a tow truck backed out into the smooth and eerily still water. Police divers looked for bodies in the area around the car and found none but they may have been pushed further out. The lake has a three-mile shoreline and they could be tangled in weeds near land.

Hearing all this, Riley sits on a rock and stares blankly at the lake.

"Their car ran over a roadside sign and left the highway over there," Harvey points up the incline. "They came through maybe 25 feet of bush and it's only about a 40-foot drop so when it landed in the water they likely would have been alive."

"What are the chances they got out?" Norman asks.

"Divers said most of the front windshield was smashed, on impact I guess. So they had a way to get out. I've seen your parents do our triathlon every year I've been here and know they're great swimmers. We found a pot and clothing and a few other things; not much though, considering they had a loaded roof rack. We'll drag the lake if we have to."

Casey says, "But if they got out, where did they go?"

"Exactly," Harvey says. "Going off the road into a lake in a storm seems a life event you'd need recovery from. Not to mention you'd wanna tell your family you're okay. Cause most people to cancel a camping trip."

"That gives me some hope," Norman says. "My parents aren't most people."

"Maybe this wasn't an accident," Casey said.

"Weather suggests it was but after yesterday it's hard to be sure about any of this," Harvey says. "By the way, Norman, has she shown you her detective license yet?"

"No. But she's okay. I mean, she's been helpful, in her own way."

Casey is pleased to hear that.

"I have to get back to the office and pass this along to Det. Sgt. Lambert in Vancouver," Harvey says. "I'll let you know of any developments. Call me if you think of anything. But do not try and solve this on your own. Leave it to us to find your family. That's our job and we're trained to do it." Harvey walks off.

It's a lot to take in and Norman looks at the incline his parents came flying down and then at the spot where the car hit the water. "It couldn't have been an accident," he suddenly tells Casey. "They know this road too well and my father is a careful driver. I don't understand how this could have anything to do with what you say you heard though. That came days later. Do you think it could be connected to Keeley and our home?"

Casey considers confessing, telling him that she only knows what she knows because she bugged a phone booth. But she doesn't want to lose her case. Or her connection. To him.

"I don't know," she tells Norman. "But it has something to do with the past, that's obvious. We need answers but first we need the right questions and it's time to start looking for them."

The tow truck pulls the Miller's car out of the water.

25.

"Oh. I see."

That's all Jack Smith has to say. Norman just told him his parents, Jack's employers, had driven off the highway and wound up submerged in Lake Still Waters and all he had to say was "Oh. I see." He said it matter-of-factly, too, and then he looked up, as if to ask if there was anything else required of him.

Norman stands over Jack's desk, Casey and Riley are by the door. The three are waiting for Jack to offer more. He does not. Finally Norman breaks the silence, "That's it?" he asks. "That's all you have to say? Because my parents may be dead, Jack."

"But you said the police didn't find their bodies."

"It's a big lake. They're still dragging it."

"Your father's a little overweight but he's active," Jack said. "Your mother is one of those power walkers and they both swim. I wouldn't jump to any conclusions. They probably swam to shore and the fact they were taking their first vacation alone in 20 years, that probably convinced them to continue on. Anyhow, I thought the paper looked quite good."

"No. Not good enough. I mean that's all you got to say about it?" Norman demands. "Why are you even here?"

Jack sighs and looks up, "What do you mean?"

"I mean why did they hire you? We ran this paper for nineteen years before you walked through that door like a Zombie and started writing bland stories and doing uninspiring lay-out.

You're about as warm as a freezing rain and it shows in everything you do."

Jack stoically takes in Norman's tirade then goes back to his computer screen. Riley, who could never get a word out of Jack and resented the new guy getting better story assignments, can't believe his brother stood up to him. His first impulse was to join in and take a shot at Jack, too, but Norman did so well he stays out of it.

Casey breaks in, "We really need to get moving."

Norman nods and grabs a key from a drawer in his desk and walks to the back of the office, unlocking a door and entering his parent's apartment. Casey follows, shaking her head dismissively as she passes Jack, and shuts the door behind her. Jack continues writing. Riley grabs his golf club and goes outside.

In his parent's apartment, Norman sits at their kitchen table.

"You okay?" Casey asks.

"Maybe I shouldn't have said those things."

"He didn't seem to care much. Come on, let's get to work. Start digging. We'll know what we're looking for when we find it."

The Miller apartment used to store junk until James and Lana had Richard O'Farrell turn it into a cozy two bedroom. From the office, you enter into the kitchen and to its right is a small bedroom, Keeley's. Straight out of the kitchen to the left is the living-room and to the right a laundry room while straight ahead is the master bedroom. Casey starts in the kitchen and tells Norman to look in the laundry for anything that raises questions. He tells her his parents don't keep secrets from him.

"Don't kid yourself," is her response. "And get looking."

In the laundry room, shelves are loaded with cleaning supplies and odds and ends and Norman, well-versed in thoroughness as a reporter, looks closely at each item before moving on to the next. He's not sure exactly what they might find but is desperate to learn something, so desperate he's willing to give over the lead in all of this to Casey. Is she hired? No, she's helping.

Casey quickly determines the kitchen has nothing of interest, ditto Keeley's room. In the master bedroom in a shelve above the coats in the closet, Casey finds a box with the word 'photos' printed on the lid. She takes it to the living-room and sits on the couch. The photos are labelled, e.g. "Norman at 3, Bluewater Park." Casey marvels at all the smiles, warmth is everywhere in these photos. There's one of Keeley taken just 2 months prior and Casey has a long look at it. It pains her to think of what Keeley must be going through.

Norman walks in, "I looked at stuff in the laundry room but couldn't find much of anything that stood out. There's cleaning stuff and tools and a baseball mitt we all took a turn at using. There is this though." He holds out a container and she puts down a photo and takes it.

"A 'Military Airtight Seal Bottle Match Case'," she reads.

"Yeah. Keeps matches dry."

"But they didn't take it."

"The wrapping said there are two match cases in the package," Norman tells her. "But there's only one there."

"So they were serious about camping and if they packed the other one and pulled it out of the water they'd be able to light a fire. That's good to know. It gives hope."

"That's what I thought."

Casey puts the container down and picks up a photo album. "I found something interesting. Look, there aren't any baby photos of you in this album, none of you younger than two. But look at this album: 'Vancouver, before Still Waters.' Is *that* you?" She points to a photo, in fading color, of a young couple on a residential street, a toddler stands between them and each of the adults is holding one of the little boy's hands.

"I've never seen this picture before but it's my parents all right," Norman is transfixed. "Little guy must be me."

"Here," she takes the photo out of the album, turns it over and reads the back. " 'Norman at 18 months, first home, 32nd Street, Vancouver.' "

"But I was born in Chilliwack. We all were. I never lived in Vancouver."

"Or so they told you. Look, there are pictures of Keeley and Riley as babies and toddlers and right up to the present, all taken in Still Waters. But while every picture of you aged two or older was taken here there are no photos of you younger than two in Still Waters. The only photo of you under two is the one in Vancouver."

She takes another picture out of the album. "And here's another one from twenty years ago, also of a couple and a toddler. But it's not the same couple. They're standing in front of the Vancouver Telegraph building."

"I've never seen the woman but I'd say the man looks like a young version of Jack Smith."

"I agree. But you said your parents have only known Jack Smith for a year."

"That's what I thought. Maybe he recently gave it to them for some reason?"

"No, it's been in this photo album a long while. See the outline where it sat?" She takes out a third photo from the album and passes it to Norman. "Now take a look at this one." The picture she hands Norman is of two young men in their late teens, standing by a school sports field and dressed in track and field garb. One holds a javelin.

"Okay, so this is the same guy from in front of the Telegraph building, the guy who looks like Jack, and he's holding a javelin and standing with my father." Norman turns the photo over and reads the caption out loud. "'*Me and Jack. Always competing, the other guy usually won. 1989.*' But if they only met last year why are they together in a photograph that's twenty years old?"

"Let's go and find out."

With all three photos in tow, they go back into the office. Jack is still at his desk. Casey drops the photo of the two young men, teenagers, in track and field garb, one identified as 'Jack,' onto Jack Smith's desk.

"Is that you?"

He hardly looks at it before passing it back to her. "Nope."

"Sure looks like you." She flips it over and points to the writing. "Same name, too."

"Jack was a popular name at one time. Bit of a resurgence lately, I understand. I do acknowledge the resemblance."

"It's you," Norman says. "And you're standing with my father."

"So you wanna tell us about it how you knew him?" Casey asks.

"Nope."

She drops down the photo of the man who appears to be a young Jack with the unidentified woman and toddler, the three standing in front of the Telegraph's building in Vancouver. Jack picks it up, glances and looks again, closer. Suddenly he's changed. He looks almost panicked, like he's just seen a ghost. He throws the photo on his desk and hastily propels his chair back and stands, glaring at Casey.

"Where the hell did you get that?" he's almost yelling.

"From a photo album in the apartment," Casey tells him, picking the picture up. "We're trying to work things out." She holds it up. "We wondered if—

"Get it away from me!" He's yelling. "Get it away I said!"

She drops the photo and he sweeps a hand across the desk, knocking it to the floor along with papers, a mug, a notebook and a pen. "God damn it!" He moves over to Norman. "They should have told you a long time ago but don't expect me to."

"I don't understand what you mean."

Jack looks at the photo on the floor and turns away, throwing his hands up over his face. "God damn it," his voice is quieter now, wracked with pain. "You leave me out of this. You hear me? Leave me out of it."

"We're just trying to find Keeley," Casey says.

Norman steps toward him. "We don't know what this is about. Obviously there's something in the past we don't know. We might not have much time."

Jack turns to Norman. "You're a reporter, Norman, and a good one. Do your background. Follow your leads. But don't ask me to be a part of this. I can't. I just can't."

He picks his notebook up from the floor and walks to the door. "God damn newspaper business," he says, dropping the notebook into the garbage.

As Riley walks in Jack walks past him and is gone.

"What happened?" Riley asks.

Norman says, "Jack got a little upset."

"Why?"

"We're not sure."

"Whatever it is," Casey says, handing a photo to Riley. "It's to do with the woman and child in this picture."

Norman picks up the land-line. "He was right – I need to do my background. I'm calling Frank Lieske, editor at the Telegraph. The one who picked up the story about our parents. We've never met but we exchange stories and talk on the phone sometimes." He reaches Lieske and puts him on speaker. Concerned, the editor asks about Keeley. He asks if Norman's parents were found and Norman tells him about the car in the lake.

Lieske says, "I'm sorry to hear that. It's awful. You know I have to do a follow-up and tie it into your sister and the mobile home being taken."

"Could you hold off?"

Frank sighs. "I can give you a day. It's a lousy thing and I feel terrible but I'll have to run something. You know that, Norman."

"Yeah. Look, Frank, I need some information. We have a reporter by the name of Jack Smith. He doesn't seem interested in the work but he's an experienced writer. I have an old photo of him standing in front of the Telegraph building and I wondered if he ever worked there."

"There was never a Jack Smith here, not that I know of."

"You sure of that?"

"I've only been here 12 years, but I'd probably have heard of him."

"Hold on." Norman puts his hand over the receiver and turns to Casey. "What letter do you claim my real surname begins with?"

"Your real surname begins with an h."

"Frank, what about a Jack with a surname that begins with an h?"

"Jack with...oh yeah. Everybody knows about Jack Hapgood."

Riley says. "Riley Hapgood? What kind of name is that?"

"He was a young reporter," Frank says. "Before my time but I know about him. In only two years he was named associate editor of news. But he developed a drinking problem and worked his way back down to a beat before being let go. His drinking started with the worst event in Telegraph history. His wife and son were killed, murdered, blown up. The idiots behind it intended to hit the wife and son of his brother, also a reporter for the Telegraph. They got their Hapgoods mixed up."

"Jesus. What was his brother's name?"

"Same first name as your Dad actually. James Hapgood. I never knew him but everyone says good things about him. Say, what's going on here? Anything I should assign a reporter to?"

"No. I, I don't know...look, I just needed some background. Thanks for your help, Frank, but I gotta go now. Thanks again."

Norman hangs up, stunned. Could this be true? Are they really Hapgoods and Jack Smith is their father's brother? That would make him their uncle. And that past is so ugly.

"Riley," Norman says. "Access the Telegraph library. Search 'Jack Hapgood' and add 'wife and son.'"

Casey asks Norman what he means by library and he explains the Telegraph library is a bank of their stories going all the way back to when the paper began publishing in 1909. Having such easy access costs but its worth it as a reference tool, especially for B.C. stories.

Riley has results. "Hey," he says. "Check this out: fifteen stories with Hapgood and the words wife and son."

"Click on one."

Riley has a story on the monitor and the three stare at the screen. "From June 23, 1996," Riley says. "Wow. Are you seeing what I'm seeing?"

Casey reads out loud: "*Local police said yesterday that last week's car bombing that killed the wife and son of Telegraph reporter Jack Hapgood was a deadly mistake. Detective Simon Curtis said police believe the bomb was intended for Lana and Norman Hapgood, the wife and son of Jack Hapgood's brother, James, also a Telegraph reporter. Detective Curtis said they believe the bombing was intended as retaliation for a series of articles James Hapgood wrote on Vernon Broom, a dooms-day prophesier and the leader of a quasi-religious sect. An employee of Broom, Earl Porter, was questioned in connection with the bombing. Police would not say if Porter will be charged.*"

"Jesus," Norman says. "My mother and I should be dead."

Riley says, "And Keeley and I shouldn't have been born."

Casey looks at the list of Cadillac owners on her phone. "Vernon Broom?" With her fingers she follows down one row, then a second and – bingo! "There's a Jerry Broom at 31 Windjammer in Vancouver. It lists a phone number." She dials. Puts her phone on speaker. A click and a message that says the number is no longer in service. "It's probably an old land line," she says.

"This is more than we can handle," Norman says. "And we agreed to tell Harvey if we found a suspect." He picks up the land line but as he dials, Casey's hand reaches in and presses the button down. She takes the phone and puts it back in the receiver.

"Harvey will take it out of our hands," she says. "Norman, he will. Look at me. We can do this. I know we can. Let's go and find your sister." Norman hesitates. "Keeley is waiting for you." Norman nods.

They head for the door.

26.

Jerry Broom and Benjie Porter sit in the black Cadillac, now rather beaten-up, at the same intersection of the Trans Canada Highway. They did not capture the Miller brothers but the intersection did produce a sighting and Jerry is confident it will do so again today.

Benjie now recognizes their situation is greatly improved, for yesterday they would not have spotted the Miller brothers if one of them hadn't gotten out of their car to throw up. Today they know what to look for: a rust-red Honda. Will they come by a second consecutive day? It seems unlikely but he was wrong before.

It is again hot and cars are again zooming by and, other than watching them, there is again little to do. Jerry has unwound the bandage he'd wrapped around his hand. He flexes it. It feels okay.

"Feels almost normal," he announces, throwing the bandage in the back seat. "I heal good."

Benjie, now reading 'Don't Sweat the Small Stuff and It's All Small Stuff,' is squeamish with what Jerry now goes back to doing. While he keeps watching the road, without looking down, Jerry is taking his gun apart and putting it back together, over and over again.

"You should be able to do this blindfolded," he says.

Benjie puts his book down. "It's disturbing. You just keep doing it. It's creepy."

Suddenly Jerry points his gun at Benjie's head.

"Think I might pull the trigger? Yeah. I just might. Right NOW!" Benjie flinches. "NOW! BANG! Ha ha. Listen: I know you don't like what we're doing but you do your job good. Yeah." He cocks the gun. "Or next time it'll be BANG for real." He smiles. "How's that martial arts training helping you now?"

Benjie could get the gun with a quick twist of his wrist but he doesn't because he doesn't think Jerry will shoot him. He lets him be the big man. This time.

"I know you the boss, Jerry. You're the man."

Jerry lowers the weapon. "Damn right I am."

Not far from them, down the highway in the direction of Still Waters, Casey Collier is driving toward Vancouver. She is not going so fast, not this time, for she wants to avoid Norman becoming car sick. He is sitting in the front seat, arms folded, staring straight ahead, and has not said a word for quite some time.

"What is it?" she finally asks. "Hey. Why has the cat got your tongue?"

"Massive cliché!" Riley bellows from the back. "Hugely massive!"

"I'm trying to get your brother to open up."

"I'm okay," Norman says. "I'm just thinking."

"I'm not going too fast am I?"

"No, you're doing fine."

"Well, something's bothering you."

"Now that you bring it up I don't think we should have brought Riley. That's been bothering me."

Riley says, "Hey, no fair!"

Casey says, "I'll keep a special eye on him. There's something else though. Out with it."

"I just keep thinking we should have called Harvey. I know what you'll say. You'll say if you want something done, you do it yourself. But I'm unsure."

"If we find her and cannot get her safely out of there then we call Harvey."

They're approaching the same intersection where the trouble started the day before. Riley looks to the roadside. "Hey. Look. Isn't that a Cadillac again?" They drive through the intersection. "Wow. It was!"

She spots the Caddy. "Shit." She guns it.

In the Cadillac, Jerry's eyes light up. The rust-red Honda has driven by the intersection, toward Vancouver this time. Engine on, tires squeal, he cranks the wheel to the right and is on the highway.

Benjie's gun is on the front seat and Jerry tells him to pick it up. "You better shoot good this time, too." Jerry says. "Aim for the tires."

Jerry sticks his gun out the window.

Casey checks her outside mirror as a bullet hits the road to the side of her door. The Caddy is closing in, getting close. Smash! – it slams into the back of the Honda, crumpling the car's rear-grill.

Riley sticks his head up and sees a dump truck coming in the other direction. "Hey, look, there's a truck up there," he says, pointing. "Let's try that again."

"You got it." Casey gives him the thumbs up, swerves into the other lane and is heading for the truck.

Seeing what she's done, Jerry reacts. "Ready for that," he mutters. He cranks his wheel to the left and he, too, veers into the other lane; he now sits in behind the Honda. The truck honks.

Casey checks her rearview and smiles. This time she won't rely on the truck avoiding her. She veers back into her correct lane.

The truck and Cadillac are on a collision course.

"Whoa!" Benjie shouts.

Jerry starts to steer back into his correct lane but there's Casey coming up alongside him; she's slowed down to occupy the space he needs to avoid the truck. She waves. He sneers and raises his gun but no time, the truck's bearing down, honking wildly. Hastily steering to the left, Jerry skids off the road and rumbles down an small embankment, slamming into an oak tree.

"Shit," he says. "Who is that woman anyhow?"

Benjie shrugs. He tries to open his door but it doesn't budge. "Could I get out your side?"

"Shut up."

27.

Norman is again talking about calling Harvey. "It's not that I don't trust you to do this," he tells Casey as they near Vancouver "I don't trust *us*. We lack resources."

When Casey asks what resources they lack he lists guns, training, officers and a car bigger than a toaster.

Twice she pulls over and asks if he wants to call Harvey for real, each time warning him that Harvey and those above him will shut them out of decisions.

"Let's say we agree to negotiate. Well, the RCMP may not allow that," she says. "We might agree to paying a ransom but they could say no. They'll set the rules."

The second time she pulls over she points out that they are nearly at the Brooms' address and that "if Keeley is there you could be minutes away from hugging her."

"Me, too," Riley says. "Though we don't normally hug."

"These guys are not an elite terrorist squad," Casey adds. "I mean they're just religious extremists without a clue what they're doing, so dumb they fly down the Trans Canada shooting guns like it's the Wild West."

"Well they got away with it," Norman says. "Twice."

"They got lucky. They obviously don't have any police-style training."

"Neither do we."

"I've been to a shooting range and I know my way around guns. Okay, that was a lie. That part of the training was later, after I quit."

"You quit?" Norman asks.

"Never mind that right now." Casey believes they could find a way to rescue Keeley but thinks Norman is more likely to go along with her if she has some useful skills to bring to the job.

"Look, we don't need a gun anyhow," she says. "I can get her out. Chinese don't need guns. If its necessary I'll use, you know, martial arts and all that."

"You're not Chinese. Not really. I'm also doubting you know any martial arts."

"Ahh, you're forgetting my parents."

"Right. Okay so how long did you last in this class?"

"Two months. Or nearly two months." She chastises herself for telling the truth but it's getting harder to lie to him.

"Great. Look, this is a pointless conversation," Norman says. "We're going there, fine, but if there are guns, and there probably will be, we're calling the RCMP."

Both times they pulled over it ended with Casey handing him her phone and telling him to go ahead and call Harvey "right now." Both times Norman handed it back.

The GPS guides them to 31 Windjammer and they park a block past the house. After she pulls over, Casey holds out her phone a final time.

"Last chance."

Norman climbs out of the car.

It's large, a two-story affair with big windows on both floors. There are eight fir trees, four on each side of the walk up. The driveway, on the left, is empty; it was extended years before to increase its size from two vehicles to four and leads to a garage big enough to hold four more.

The home faces a bluff on the other side of the street that runs down to a beach. It's an expensive home but the neighbourhood is no longer exclusive and is only a block away from an area that includes apartment buildings and stores.

Looking at the home, Norman's heart sinks. There are no lights and no signs of life. Adding to the look of abandonment is a large oak desk on the front lawn, complete with a chair. Full darkness is not far away and the desk and approaching night add an air of desertion to the property. Norman senses they are not going to find his sister there. A part of him wants to immediately get back in the car and look somewhere else. But where?

Riley walks into the yard and sits at the desk and rifles through drawers, finding a pamphlet, which he puts in a pocket, along with a pen and a blank sheet of paper, the pen and paper he drops on the desk. That's all the desk contains.

From a vantage point crouching behind a tree at the side of the yard, Casey and Norman are looking up at the house and at first don't see Riley sitting at the desk. Once she sees him, Casey rushes over and grabs his shoulder.

"You're in plain view," she whispers.

She takes the pen and paper and stuffs them in her pocket and pulls Riley along, motioning Norman to follow. They creep down the right side of the house. At the first window, she reaches up to check the latches.

"I don't think anybody's home," Riley says.

"We don't know that for sure," Casey says. "So keep your eyes open."

"Unless I'm sleeping I keep my eyes open."

Norman says, "Dummy up with the smart aleck stuff, Riley, or I'll club you one. And I don't wanna hear the word cliche for awhile."

Casey whispers, "Could you two keep quiet please?"

Finding the latch at the bottom of the window, she tries to push it up but it won't budge. She cautiously makes her way further along the side of the home. Sticking her hand up to a second window, Casey finds the latch and pushes...but no, it too is locked. She moves on to a third window and again tries the latch. Locked again. Oops, she knocks a pair of grass clippers from the ledge and they fall to the ground with a thud. A light comes on in the window's room and Casey and Norman dive to the grass. The window is flung open and leaning forward and looking down – is Riley.

"I picked the lock on the front door," he says. "Come on in, it's open." He disappears back inside.

"How does he learn stuff like that?" Norman asks, as they pick themselves up.

"Just be glad he does."

The two backtrack to the front. Casey looks at a notice tacked onto the door; there's just enough light to read it. She says, "Check this out: *This home is being seized due to non-payment of taxes...goods forfeited...*etcetera etcetera *by order of Municipal Judge Reveer Doshi.* So right after they lose their house, they steal yours."

They step inside.

They are in a very large home, spacious and stylish, a mansion. To the left of the entrance is a door that leads to the room formerly used by Reverend Broom for his office. A passageway continues to the back of the house. To the right, on the other side of the entrance, is a large opening to a living-room while directly in front of them is a winding staircase that has Casey thinking of a 50s Betty Davis movie.

Riley stands at the top of the stairs, idly hanging his arms over the railing.

"It's pretty cool," he calls down. "No furniture but lots of rooms. I'm checking to see if Keeley is here." He walks along the landing toward a room. Norman calls out for him to come down but Riley is gone.

"He doesn't listen."

"Did you listen when you were a teenager?" Casey asks.

"I did actually, yes."

"I'll look up there. You check around down here. She's probably still in your home hidden somewhere but let's look around while we're here." Casey goes up the stairs.

Norman walks into Reverend Broom's office. It's now just an unoccupied room with no furniture and a disconnected land-line on the floor next to a crumbled piece of paper. He picks up the paper, another copy of the notice about seizing the home and contents. He can't know the desk on the front lawn, left because there was no room in the final load and forgotten, sat in this room for years. He throws the paper down.

Upstairs Casey and Riley walk through mostly empty rooms. Riley hands her a pamphlet called *The Explosives Handbook: How to Blow Things Up.*

"Where did you get this?"

"It was in that desk in the front yard."

In one room, they find a bookcase with titles like *Rise up with Our Savior* and *Worship God and He Won't Leave You Behind.* Many combine money and God, such as *Donating Money in God's Name* and *Giving to your Ministry: A Pathway to Salvation.* There are books on the Jonestown massacre in Guyana, others on Waco and Ruby Ridge. Pamphlets on preparing for the end by donating to The Holy Broom Foundation are stacked against a wall.

Another room is empty save for two piles of books. Riley sits on one pile and begins leafing through the books in the other.

Casey says, "I'll go see what your brother's doing."

Alone downstairs Norman stands at the entrance to the living-room. It's a large space but there's nothing in it except a coffee table. He hears something and turns to find a small dog staring at him. It's the Pekingese, The Dog That Bites Jerry.

Norman loves dogs, something he is reluctant to show the world, but if there are no humans around he often speaks to dogs and cats in a high-pitched voice, a falsetto, which he believes is low-status and friendly; he uses the same voice when talking to very small children and the extreme elderly. Secretly he loves the idea of being one of those people that children, old people and pets adore. Has he succeeded? Not so much.

"Oh, hi there little doggie," he says in his falsetto voice. "Nice to see you today." A low growl. "Come on. Be nice." Another growl. "Who's a good boy? Huh?"

The Dog That Bites Jerry curls its little lips and looks ready to snap; Norman slowly moves his hand back.

"That was a cute voice." Casey is at the bottom of the stairs. "You should use it more often."

"Very funny. I was just trying to see if it was friendly," Norman says. "It doesn't seem to be."

"It's a Pekingese," Casey tells him. "Don't be fooled by their size, they can be vicious. Sleeps in there I'd bet." She points to a closet near the living-room entrance with a small entrance flap at the bottom. Casey opens it, finds a blanket covered in dog hair and two empty bowls. The dog goes over to Casey, who crouches and

166

sticks out her hand. The Dog That Bites Jerry licks it.

Norman says, "Seems to like you well enough."

"Pets, toddlers and really old people love me."

"Oh yeah? Nice, if you care about that sort of thing."

"Any sign your sister was here?"

"Doesn't seem to be, no."

"Kitchen is probably along that passage on the other side of the stairs. I'll see if there's anything for her to eat. She's a she; looks like they abandoned her. Jerks."

The dog follows Casey past the office and down a passageway into a large kitchen with a shiny metal double fridge and self-regulating stove. There are cupboards with plates and cups, others with food, the room hasn't been emptied. Casey finds dog crunchies and puts some in a bowl, sets it on the floor and the dog attacks it.

Casey hoists herself up on a counter and pulls out the paper and pen Riley found. "I think I'm gonna make the first entry in my notes about you." She writes, speaking out loud as she goes. "A *small hungry female dog found in the abandoned Broom home. Likes me better than client; I think she senses his fear.* How's that for journalism, Norman?" She frowns and keeps writing: *No sign of Keeley.*"

In the living-room, Norman finds nothing in the coffee table and walks back toward the staircase. He hears something outside and stiffens. A car door? He cautiously opens the front door, a sliver. Night has come on and he can't see much; he starts to close the door when the muzzle of a gun slides through the opening.

"Got 'cha," Jerry says. "Dummy. Now back up."

The gun pointed at his chest, Norman moves back and the

younger Broom opens the door wide and steps inside, indicating by flicking his gun that Norman should keep moving back.

Benjie follows and closes the door.

"Do we have to brandish gun?" Benjie asks. Jerry looks confused. "Do we have to *use* guns?" Benjsie says.

Jerry says, "If you want people to do things they don't wanna do, it comes in handy."

"Where's my sister?" Norman asks, doing his best to sound like he's not terrified.

"In her room, where else?" Jerry says. "Ha-ha."

"You better not hurt her."

Benjie says, "She's okay, trust me."

Jerry says, "For now she is."

Casey picks this moment to walk out the kitchen door and start down the passage. When she sees Jerry and the gun she hastily turns back. Too late.

"Stop or I shoot," Jerry says. "Over here."

Casey walks out and stands next to Norman. "I guess you're Jerry Broom."

"You got that right. Came to get my Dad's dog but getting you guys is way better. You're the race driver of that minature Honda."

"You know we gave this address to the police," she lies. "They're on their way."

"I doubt that. You should have only you figured you could rescue her by yourself. Now where's the kid?"

"You missed him," Casey says. "Dropped him at my aunt's; they're flying to the Shanhai Pass in China to visit the Great Wall."

"That's another lie."

"Serious, vacation of a lifetime."

Jerry says, "Benjie, take your gun out and go look upstairs for the kid"

Pulling his gun out of the back of his pants, Benjie heads up the staircase. In the third room he checks he finds Riley, now sitting on the second stack of books and looking through the first stack.

"Hey." Benjie smiles, lowering his gun. "How's it going?"

"Oh. Wow. Hi. That's a gun."

"Yeah. But I probably don't have bullets left; I wouldn't shoot anyhow. My name is Benjie Porter."

"I'm Riley Mil...Riley Hapgood. Was that you shooting at us in the Cadillac?"

"Yes. I missed on purpose."

"Was it much fun?"

"Was what much fun?"

"Shooting a gun."

"I didn't get much out of it, to be honest."

Riley says, "This is a pretty big house."

"Its Reverend Broom's. Or was. It's finally been foreclosed after years of court battles."

"Why are you chasing us?"

"Uhm, it's to do with revenge. I find the logic hard to follow. The Reverend likes getting revenge, like he's obsessed with it." Benjie would like to change the subject. "I see you found something to read. I read a lot." He sits on the stack of books next to the stack Riley sits on.

Riley says, "These are on religious cults." He passes the book he was holding to Benjie. "This one's about the Jonestown massacre. Did you know over 900 people died there?"

Benjie puts his gun down and opens the book. He says, "Oh yeah. I was brought up on this stuff."

"So you know about Ruby Ridge and the shootout at Waco, Texas in 1993?"

"My Dad was there; so was Reverend Broom; that's where they met."

"At Waco? During the FBI siege?"

"They left two days before that. They argued with the leaders of the sect so Reverend Broom left to get revenge by starting his own religion. See what I mean by the Reverend and revenge? Anyhow, he and my Dad snuck out of Waco in the dead of night." Benjie puts the book down. "The history books don't know about that."

"It's cool your dad was there."

"Yeah, Reverend Broom and my Dad were Seventh-day Adventist then but they believed in the rapture."

"I've heard of that. Everybody flies up to heaven."

"Yeah. It's a lifting up to the heavens but only true Christians get to go. They also believe in the second coming, like the Branch Davidians at Waco. Most of us Christians believe in that. But the Reverend said the rapture and second coming will only happen when he's the supreme religious leader. He says if you don't believe that you won't get raptured."

"What happens to you then?"

"You get left behind and die a horrible death. "

"Huh. Nice."

"The people at Waco thought the Reverend was a false prophet but not my father. If Reverend Broom said the Earth was filled with pancakes, he'd start eating."

"That's weird."

Benjie nods. "Yeah. He was a long-haul trucker from Utah delivering religious icons to the compound in Waco. He met the Reverend and the rest is history." Riley resists telling Benjie 'the rest is history' is a massive cliché.

"They came to Canada and my father met my mother," Benjie continues. "Or they met on a religious dating site and he brought here from the Philippines. She died of cancer two years ago."

"That really sucks."

"Yeah. I miss her pretty bad."

"But I guess you got, you know, your religion to help you feel better."

"I know I'll see her again, so yeah that helps. I'm a strong believer though I'm not sure about the rapture. I like our congregation, or most things about it. The Reverend Broom makes everyone give their worldly possessions to him and pay tithes. That I don't like."

"I think all cult leaders get around to saying you have to do that."

"After the Reverend bought a mansion a lot of the congregants asked for their money back but he said he spent it all on the Lord's work. This newspaper wrote stories that said he was a thief and people started leaving and some of them took him to court."

"I think my father wrote those stories."

"That's what this is about. My Dad kept copies and I've read them. Your Dad did his research."

Riley says. "You know what? I thought you'd be different. Like bad. But you seem normal. Except for the gun and it doesn't have bullets."

"*Probably* it doesn't, I said. It might. I really didn't count how many times I fired it."

"The point is you don't seem so bad. Or bad at all."

"Thanks," he tells Riley. "But watch out because there's a *real* bad guy down there. The Reverend Broom's son. He's unbalanced and I'm not sure what he'll do if things don't go his way."

A voice from downstairs. It's Jerry wondering what's taking so long. "Speak of the devil," Benjie says.

Riley again resists noting the cliché.

Benjie picks up his gun and goes out to the landing. "I captured a drought-bringer," he yells down. "I'll bring him down."

He hustles back into the room and picks up his gun. "I have to take you downstairs," he tells Riley. "If I don't he'll come up here and you don't want that. I'll do what I can for you guys and I won't let him hurt you."

Riley gets up. Benjie says, "Act like you're nervous of me. Maybe act, you know, afraid of me."

"Easy. I'll just act like my brother."

Downstairs, Jerry has Casey and Norman sitting on the coffee table in the living-room and he's asked the whereabouts of Norman's parents. Norman tells him their car was found in Lake Still Waters and that they are almost certainly dead.

"So our family is going through a lot," he says. "Look, you can keep the motor home. Just let my sister go."

"Your so-called home isn't going anywhere ever again. This is about your father's lies. He thought he got away with them but the Lord works in mysterious ways."

Benjie is down the stairs, his gun jammed into Riley's back. "I got the kid, Jerry."

Riley says, "This guy is real scary."

"Finally you do your job," Jerry pulls out his phone. "Good stuff. Now watch these people while I phone my father. And keep up the good work."

A low growl from a dog. Jerry hastily puts his phone back in his jacket. "You hear that? The beast," he says. "I better find her. You keep an eye on these people."

He steps out of the living-room and walks to the dog's closet. Empty. As he turns around, the dog, snarling, charges out at Jerry from behind the banister. Jerry raises his gun but the dog leaps and clenches its jaws on his right hand. The gun flies out of his grasp and skids across the floor.

The Dog That Bites Jerry dashes back in the direction of the kitchen, disappearing through the open door.

"Ahh. Shit. Wretched beast! Christ!"

The gun has come to rest on the floor ten feet from Casey; she is up and takes a step toward it.

"Shoot her." Jerry cries, clutching his bleeding hand.

Benjie points his gun at Casey and she freezes. The two are staring at one another as Riley casually walks over to Jerry's gun and picks it up.

He points it at Jerry.

Riley says, "Benjie likes books. He also didn't reload so his gun is probably, not for certain but he said *probably*, out of bullets."

"You told him you were out of bullets?" Jerry asks.

173

"No. Not exactly. As he just said, I told him I was probably out. I didn't count or look in the...whatever."

Jerry says, "It's called the chamber."

Casey holds her hand out to Riley. "Give it to me. I'm a professional."

Norman says, "I don't think she is but, yeah, best to give her the gun. Now please, Riley."

Reluctantly, Riley hands Casey the gun. She points it at Jerry

"You don't know guns." Jerry says to Casey as he walks over and takes Benjie's gun and points it at her. "But me? Me, I know guns real good."

"Only you have no bullets," Casey says.

Benjie says, "He might actually."

"Just tell us where Keeley is and we can all go home." Casey says. "Or Vancouver's rental market isn't great but I'm sure you'll find something."

"Here's a better idea," Jerry says. "Give me my gun back and I don't shoot you."

"You really wanna risk a shoot out?"

"Oh, I like risks."

"He does seem to enjoy them," Benjie says.

Casey says, "You pull that trigger and nothing comes out there's no way I miss from twenty feet."

"But something might come out."

"You know what? I think we'll go and we can argue about this another day."

Nodding to the brothers, Casey begins backing out of the room, the gun she holds fixed on Jerry. Norman nods to Riley and they slowly move backwards. Jerry cautiously follows.

Casey, Riley and Norman near the front door, their backs to it. With deliberation, for his right hand is bleeding from the most recent dog bite, Jerry pulls the hammer back on Benjie's gun. He likes the effect.

Norman steps in front of his brother. The tragedies overtaking his family have created a singular thought in his mind: "*I must protect Riley.*"

Casey could shoot and be done with Jerry but if there's a bullet left in Benjie's gun he might be able to get a shot off before going down. Having never fired a gun, despite how close he is to her, she also realizes she may not even hit him. She also worries about Keeley, killing Broom's son would further fuel his thirst for revenge and she'd be the one to pay the price.

As for Riley, as he inches toward the door he remembers that somewhere in all of the books he has read he encountered the word 'fatalism' and he decides to embrace it, to be a fatalist.

He turns and bolts out the door.

Emboldened by his kid brother, Norman turns and runs. Jerry Broom has had enough and fires at Norman's retreating figure: *click*. No bullets. Norman is out.

Casey has a free pass to take Jerry out.

"You don't have the guts," he says.

She stands, frozen. It's not just fear for Keeley that stops her from pulling the trigger. She realizes that killing just isn't her thing.

"Maybe another time," she says, and is out the door.

Jerry methodically takes bullets from his pocket and starts to reload Benji's gun.

As they run down the driveway, Norman and Casey unknowingly pass Riley, crouched in the dark near the Cadillac's right front tire, pocketknife in hand. He jams at the tire but the knife's too small, the tire too thick.

His brother and Casey creep along the sidewalk in front of the house, softly calling for him, but Riley ignores them and keeps trying to puncture the tire.

Yard lights suddenly come on and illuminate the driveway. Jerry and Benjie are coming down the walkway. Riley is easily visible and Jerry trains his gun on him.

"Drop the knife and stand up," he tells Riley. Riley drops the knife and Benjie picks it up. Jerry opens the trunk and takes out some rope, flings Riley against the side of the car and, as Casey and Norman watch from the neighbouring yard, ties Riley's hands together.

"Throw him in the back seat," he tells Benjie. "And don't screw up or I'll shoot you both."

Benjie grabs Riley. Under his breath he tells him: "You should have kept running." Opening the rear door, he slides Riley in and gets into the passenger seat. Jerry takes a final look around and jumps into the driver's side, giving Benjie his gun back and grabbing another from the glove box.

"Not so smart telling him you didn't reload."

He starts the car. Benjie reminds him they came to get the dog. "My father'll be happy with what we got," Jerry says. "Two kids down only one more to go."

In the backseat, Riley silently enumerates the things he is feeling and his list is long: angry, mad, pissed, alone, annoyed and, surprisingly given his situation, hungry.

But not afraid, not Riley.

Crouched behind a red elderberry bush in the neighbouring yard are Casey and Norman. As the Cadillac backs out of the driveway, Norman is determined to act.

He says. "Give me the gun."

"No. It's too risky. You could hit Riley."

"So what do we do then?"

"I don't know."

"You don't know?" he hisses. "You were supposed to be watching him!"

"I'm sorry. It was dark. I didn't see him. What was he doing there anyways?"

"Now you're blaming him? He's a kid!"

"Okay, okay, stay down." She creeps around the edge of the bush and slips in behind a tree and trains her gun on the Caddy as it pulls into the street. She can't clearly make out anyone though.

Jerry steps on the gas.

Gun raised, Casey stands but can only watch as the Cadillac speeds off. It reaches the end of the block and turns a corner and is gone. Flopping against the tree, she slides down, sitting with her back against it.

"Some detective you are," Norman says, standing over her. "You can't even keep a 13-year-old boy safe."

"You're right. I'm sorry."

He just shakes his head, sighs, starts off in the direction of the corner the Cadillac disappeared around.

Casey follows.

"I know it doesn't do any good but it was my bad," she calls out to him. "I hate that phrase. I should have kept a closer eye on him. I'm the professionl."

"You're not a professional."

"Listen: we can't give up. I won't give up. Never. We'll get them back, I promise. I mean, you know, if you want something done in this world you gotta do – "

Norman turns to her: "I've have had my fill of that particular phrase, thank you. And of you. I'm going to the police. And that's something I can do myself." He starts walking, half-muttering to himself, half-talking to her. "I should have never listened to you. Christ."

He suddenly turns. "All right. Okay. Wait. Listen. I'll give you one more chance. You can lend me your phone to call the police."

"My battery's dead, actually."

"Jesus. You're pathetic," he walks off again.

"There's a phone booth across the street from my apartment."

He stops and turns. "Tell me something," he says, walking backwards and away from her as he rants. "How many of my family are left? Four? Huh? Three? Two? No. Not even one. They're *all* gone."

He keeps walking. She says "hold on" and runs back to the Honda and drops the gun in her shoulder bag then catches up to Norman as he reaches the corner.

They are on a busy street in the Kitsilano area of Vancouver. It's Friday night and there's a steady stream of cars and pedestrians. Norman takes in the noise and the endless bustle. This is his first view of a busy metropolis at night and, overwhelmed, he becomes rooted to his spot on the sidewalk.

Casey gingerly approaches. "Are you okay?"

"No, I don't think I am."

Two men quarrel as they walk by, something about a deal gone bad. A woman pushing a shopping cart of old clothes, dishes, small bags, moves quickly past. A bunch of teen boys give each other high-fives and laugh.

Norman mutters, "Where could they be going hey?"

Casey shrugs. "Just living their lives. Like all of us."

"How do you do it?" he calls out to passersby. "How do you tolerate the traffic and lights and the bleeping noise?" Most people rush on, ignoring him, but some stop and watch the minor spectacle. "There's too many of you," Norman loudly says. "And you don't even know each other."

She gently grabs his shoulder, "Hey, maybe we should find a bench. Figure out a strategy."

He quickly turns to her. "No. I've had enough of this doing things, of all this action. I'm gonna report Riley's kidnapping to the police and then I'm going home to wait for my family."

A taxi comes their way and Norman waves his arms and yells: "Hey Cabbie!" The cab draws up and Norman opens the back door and jumps in. Casey is at the window and he slams his hand on the lock and then leans into the front, locking that door, too. He rolls down his window half-way. "One more thing: you're fired," he tells her. "Step on it, driver."

The cab speeds off.

The people move off and Casey is left alone on the corner. She takes in what just went down, it begins to sink in that Riley and Keeley are in deep trouble and that she is alone and doesn't know how to help them.

Time to go... but where?

She starts walking back to Philip's car. She hears a noise, a whimpering, and sees The Dog That Bites Jerry staring pleadingly up at her. She leans down and extends her arm toward it and the Pekingese licks her hand.

"Come on," Casey says. "Let's go."

Together, the two walk off down the street.

28.

Det. Sgt. Reg Lambert is on his mobile. A veteran officer, over-weight, bald, two years from retirement but sharp and genuine, he paces behind his desk as he talks, occasionally leaning down and making a note on a pad that sits amongst the clutter upon his desk.

Norman is sitting, he's just finished his written account of the events at the former Broom mansion and is waiting for the detective. Lambert hangs up and is back in his seat.

"Okay, I have officers checking that house now. Also, I'm told they've changed vehicles," Lambert says. "A damaged black Cadillac, matches your description, turned up a few blocks from the house. No report of a stolen vehicle in the area but one is sure to surface when the owner goes to use it. No telling when that might be so until then we won't know what they're driving."

Norman slides the paper he'd written on across the desk, negotiating around files, a stapler and the program for yesterday's horse races at Hastings Park. "I wrote it all down."

"Great," Lambert has a quick look. "That's quite the experience you had. You shouldn't have done what you did but let's not get into that. Your intentions were good and you helped our investigation, no question. Obviously the outcome wasn't what we wanted."

"So what do I do now?"

"You don't do anything. Go home. We'll check Broom's associates, where he held his meetings, things like that. We been working with Cpl. Kwong and I'll let him know about Riley. His officers collected shell casings off the highway but we couldn't match the weapon to any crime. And no luck finding your motor home or Keeley."

"It's a big home."

"There's a lot of forested land between here and Still Waters and that's where we intend to start looking now. Hey, we're gonna find these guys. But you have to leave it up to us. You write down your number?"

"I don't have a mobile but you can call the newspaper. You don't think he'll hurt them, do you? They're kids. They've never done anything to anyone."

Lambert sighs. "Those killings, your Aunt and cousin, I was here then. These guys are not your typical religious nuts. They are obviously very dangerous."

"So what will you do?"

"We have options. I'll work on getting a chopper up and increase the number of officers on the case. So unless you have any more questions I should make some calls." Norman, a bit overwhelmed, shakes his head. The detective stands and the two shake shake hands. "You hang in there and call me anytime, day or night."

Unsure where the bus depot is, soon after leaving the police station Norman finds himself on a darkly lit street in a part of town peopled by the less fortunate. In Still Waters the less-fortunate are not as less-fortunate as these are. Sirens wail. A man sleeps on the sidewalk with cardboard for a blanket. Rough looking teens smoking what is surely marijuana. He trips over a young couple slumped against an empty store front with two Rottweilers and a sign asking for dog food money; Norman timidly drops in a few coins.

A block from the station he gets a pizza slice and sits on a bench. He could not live in this environment, he tells himself again. But he's glad to finally experience it.

The Pacific Central Station is also where trains depart and though it's nearly midnight by the time he finds his way there, twenty-five or so people are milling about, buying tickets, talking, sitting or sleeping on benches. City bus depots at night can be unnerving – Norman sees a guy with a weasel on his head – but he bears up as best he can. After visiting the men's room he gets into a ticket line-up, third from the front.

As he waits he takes out his notebook: *Screwed up. Riley taken. Alone. City is dark and people in bus depot unusual; washroom needs cleaning*. He makes notes about the dog, his rant to Casey on the city street, his visit to the police station and his fear for Keeley and Riley. Second in line now, an elderly couple speaking in Punjabi are in front of him. He keeps writing.

"I made notes, too." It's Casey, standing behind him. "I been sitting on a bench and writing about being shot at and about Riley and how I screwed up. It felt cathartic to write things down. I could get used to it."

Norman puts his notebook away and stares straight ahead. Stubborn man.

"I was nervous about how you would react so I watched you. Did some thinking. I should have kept a better eye on Riley and shouldn't have talked you out of calling Harvey. I had no business doing this on my own."

Norman looks at her. He knows it wasn't all her fault. "I could have called him. It was a longshot but I chose to go there with you and let Riley come with us."

"I have something in my notes I'd like to share." She pulls out a piece of paper. "Here we go: *Time to admit to Norman that I am not a detective*. That's it. I'm a fraud; I've been lying; I'm not a detective; I never was."

"That isn't exactly a surprise."

"I took a course but dropped out. Most of the course content was investigating insurance fraud and tailing spouses." The Punjabi-speaking couple are being served now. "Dropping out was nothing new, I don't tend to finish things. Except for a shift. I do marketing surveys. I talk for a living."

"That isn't exactly a surprise, either."

"I planted a bug in a phone booth. Unethical, I know. But I wanted a case and figured people who still use phone booths are more likely to be criminals avoiding being tracked. My logic was faulty but I got the result I was looking for. I now believe what I heard was Earl Porter telling Vernon Broom about the story Riley wrote. It was clear they intended to find you. I couldn't be sure what it was about but they weren't nice people, that much I knew. Yes, I could have been more open with the police, and you, but what I had was vague and the more time I spent with you and Riley the more I wanted to help. So I kept my mouth shut."

"It's a peculiar thing to want to do. Eavesdrop and slink your way into people's lives."

"I grew up in a household that lacked excitement."

"You said so already."

"Look, I'd like to finish this and providing we tell Harvey anything we learn this time, we might be able to help find them." Norman is up at the ticket window.

Casey says, "The next bus to Still Waters doesn't leave until 7:55 a.m."

"You're a walking bus schedule."

"That's why they have schedules, you know, so you can look up the times and plan accordingly. Not being a bus guy I guess you wouldn't know that. Sorry."

Norman ignores her and pays for a ticket to Still Waters and walks over to a bench and sits. She sits next to him. He looks at his ticket and sees she's right, the bus doesn't leave until 7:55 a.m. He sighs.

"You're welcome to sleep at my place," she says. "I owe you. Couch is small, you'll have to bend your legs but it's that or spend the night with this lot." She looks around. "See the guy with a weasel on his head?" She points at the man with the weasel and he sees her pointing and waves. "Seems like a nice guy, actually. Not everyone here is though. Two assaults in the last month."

Norman realizes he'll get no sleep in a bus depot.

Ten minutes later, he walks into Casey's apartment and is greeted by The Dog That Bites Jerry.

"I named her Vicious," Casey tells him. "I'm not sure she likes men."

Vicious smells Norman and looks up at him. He puts his hand down and she licks it; he pets her and rubs her ear.

Casey says, "She must remember the cute voice at the house. Coffee or tea? I got a local craft beer, too."

"A beer, thanks." He sits on the couch, a two-seater. He looks around. It's not a big place but he notices how clean and tidy she keeps it. Nothing on her walls but there are knickknacks on the shelves. No stuffies, which in Norman's eyes is a positive.

She hands him a beer, drops a package of Viva Puff cookies on the coffee table and sits next to him.

"Did you call Harvey?"

"No but I went to the police and filled out forms and told the detective about Riley. He's gonna tell Harvey."

"What did the detective say?"

"Not much. He said they've abandoned the Cadillac so police don't know what they're driving now. They can't find the motor home. It seems hopeless."

Casey longs to reach out and sooth him. Hold on to him. She wonders why this keen-eyed, small-town reporter who shuns the modern world seems to be the one who can help her feel whole. When he left in the cab she worried her case, him, was over. The bus depot was her last chance. The easy part was waiting. Sitting here talking to him is the hard part. Her throat is constricted and she's not used to her heart beating so quickly.

"It's not hopeless," she says. Next, without thinking about it, without warning, she hears her voice say, "Do you ever get lonely?"

He wasn't expecting that. Not sure how to answer. So he doesn't say anything.

She plunges on, "I mean does having a big and wonderful family like you do make you feel whole?" Still nothing. "You don't have to answer that."

She stands and takes something down from a small shelf behind the couch, a pair of colorful, delicately woven, wool baby shoes. She hands them to him.

"I was a month old. Left in a basin at the door of a community center in a city called Shantou, with these on. Not uncommon in China at the time, baby girls left in basins. These shoes are the only material connection I have to my birth mother. I believe she must have made them for me. Whenever I feel lonely I hold on to them."

After a moment he speaks, softly, "They're lovely," he says. "The colors are beautiful."

"Yeah."

"They were made with love. That's evident."

"You think so?"

He does and nods his head. "Yeah. It must have been hard for her."

"It was the culture. I know that. Male preferenced, male dominated. Whatever."

"Do you think about her much?"

"A lot sometimes. I mean I have a mother but I think about this one. I would have liked to have had a picture of her." She takes the shoes. "Anyhow, sorry to get sentimental on you."

"Not at all. Thank you for showing them to me."

She returns the shoes to the shelf and sits back down. "Here's my final confession of the night." she says. "I feel alive around your family in a way I don't around my own. I feel connected." Here we go, she thinks, the big reveal. "I feel connected to you. It's a lousy time I know so you can ignore that. I'm not even sure why I said it."

In the quiet, Casey mentally berates herself. This is not how she behaves and it's not the right time for him. But she realizes that only by holding him and being held by him can she relax.

She wants to invite him into her bedroom.

Norman breaks the silence, "I feel wrong about doing anything. Not that you were suggesting anything. I mean I feel wrong about even breathing. About drinking this beer or sitting comfortably. It's like I should be a catatonic. Like I shouldn't do anything but worry and be afraid for them. I hate how life goes on and they could be anywhere and in terrible distress. But it's better to be with someone. It's better to be with you."

He leans to her and, side by side, they embrace.

She stands and walks to her bedroom; in the doorway she turns back. "If you want company it's a queen size bed and you might actually get some sleep." Pushing it. "It's up to you."

She leaves the door ajar.

Norman takes a drink. He finds himself thinking how he enjoyed watching Casey undress in his yard. It wasn't so much a leering enjoyment, though there was that, but it was something more. Through her bedroom door he can make out her shadow on the wall as she undresses and gets into bed. He stands.

By her bed now, he removes his clothes and pulls the covers back. She's been watching and you could have offered her the lead on every case that Sherlock Holmes and Dr. Watson never got around to solving and she would have turned them down to lie there and watch Norman Hapgood get into her bed. She reaches her hand out and feels for his. They hold hands, lying on their backs. Suddenly he rolls over to his side toward her and now they hold one another.

"I'd like to go to sleep like this," is what he says.

"Yes please."

Vicious, who sits on her haunches in the doorway watching, whimpers and turns and walks over to the couch, hops up, lays down and closes her eyes.

Together, Casey and Norman fall asleep.

29.

It is the middle of the night and Riley is bound and gagged. At last he is scared but there's no one he can tell that to and, in any case, it would be hard to fit another human into the trunk of the 1977 Ford Mercury Marquis he has been stuffed into.

He isn't sure how long he's been in there. When they arrived at the clearing where the motor home is hidden, Jerry dragged him out of the stolen car, hands tied behind his back and a gag over his mouth, and sat him against a tree. In the light of the moon Riley saw his home for the first time since leaving it after delivering peach juice and a raspberry muffin to his sister two mornings ago. It was a shock to see it there.

He knew Keeley was inside and struggled to stand and get to her. Jerry had grabbed him by the throat. "You wanna make sure she isn't hurt then don't do anything stupid," he said. As he was pushed back down, Riley saw Benjie standing a few feet away.

Jerry turned and walked toward the motor home. "Watch him," he told Benjie on his way past him. "And make sure that you do your job good." Riley watched Jerry open the door and enter his home.

Benjie moved to Riley and leaned down. "I can't help you now," he said, *sotto voce*. "But I'll watch out for you."

The door to the house opened and Benjie straightened up as Reverend Broom and his son came out and they walked over to the tree.

Reverend Broom stood over Riley. Riley thought the guy was

trying to make like he was royalty but came off looking like a phony. Broom knelt down and reached out to touch Riley gently on the cheek.

"My son tells me your father is perished," he said. "Your brother is now the head of your family and he must be the one to bear witness. So I need you to link you together with your sister tomorrow."

Broom reminded Riley of a Hollywood actor from a long time ago, Vincent Price, who he'd seen in horror movies at his friend Arjun's. Tall and gaunt with a deep, eerie voice. What a jerk, Riley thought, and what a lot of gibberish was coming out of his mouth.

Broom told his son to take the gag off the prisoner and Jerry knelt and ripped the grey duct tape off. The Reverend told Riley he had a role to play and asked if he was ready to be sacrificed so his father could "atone" for the destruction of his ministry.

"Yeah, I can't wait," Riley answered. "God, what a dumb question."

It is true Riley does not tolerate clichés but in that moment he thought of producing one himself. He thought what a terrible cliché it would be if he were to spit in the face of this man. The old 'spit in the face to show how tough he was' trick. One of the worst movie clichés ever, Riley thought, right out of almost every second-rate Hollywood crime drama he had ever seen. But, he reasoned, it would still be fun.

"Pa-tooey!"

A big load of gob right in Reverend Broom's face. It landed on an eye and rolled down his cheek until it fell upon his suit jacket. Reverend Broom recoiled, lurching back while muttering imprecations and threats. Jerry stepped forward and clobbered Riley on the side of his head, then aimed a kick to his ribs. Standing nearby, Benjie had an impulse to take out Jerry right there.

But he did nothing. Jerry grabbed Riley by the hair and stood him up, pulling him over to his father, who was wiping his face with a handkerchief.

"What you want me to do with him?"

"Put his gag back on and throw the varmint in the trunk."

And that is how Riley ended up where he is now.

He is miserable and angry in there. Keeping himself occupied by thinking of what he'd do to Jerry if he got the chance. It would be fun to lock Jerry in a pen with a pack of pit bulls, he thought. That would be so awesome.

As those images were being broadcast into Riley's half-asleep brain at 2 a.m. he heard a noise. Benjie again? Twice already Benjie had opened the trunk to check on Riley. Tucked into his bed on the ground behind a rock, Benjie couldn't sleep knowing a teenage boy was stuffed into the trunk of a car fifty feet away. He was plagued by that and by thoughts of the girl and of not knowing what Reverend Broom intended to do.

Benjie's conscience kept impelling him to check on Riley. The first time he opened the trunk, Riley kicked him in his ribs. The second time Benjie told Riley he was concerned there wasn't enough air. Riley pretended to be suffocating and when Benjie leaned closer, he head-butted him. Benjie closed the trunk and tried to sleep again but still no luck.

He opens the trunk a third time.

"I'm gonna take your gag off," Benjie says. "If you yell it will wake them and that won't help you or your sister. I have juice. We could talk. So don't yell. Promise?"

Riley nods yes. Benjie leans in. If the kid was going to kick or head-butt him again, so be it, at least he'd know Riley wasn't going to co-operate and perhaps that knowledge would help him get to sleep.

Riley doesn't move as Benjie takes the duct tape into his hand and gently pulls. Gentle doesn't work. "Sorry, I'm going to have to pull harder." He yanks it harder. Worked. Must have hurt though. "Sorry."

A bit too loudly, Riley says, "At the house you told me you were a friend."

"Shh, keep it down. I am your friend."

"So let me get my sister and get out of here."

"It's not that simple. I have to talk my father out of this."

"But he killed my aunt and cousin."

"That's not true. My mother believed a man named Bud Clement killed them and I do, too. I can make my father understand revenge and destruction have nothing to do with God's will. If I can make him see that I'm certain he'll help me end this."

"You go ahead. I mean I don't care what you do to stop this. But you better do it fast."

"I promise I won't abandon you."

"I'm only thirteen but already I'm aware most people are better at promising things than they are at doing them."

"Trust me. It's the only way." He puts the gag back over Riley's mouth. "I'm sorry." He closes the trunk and goes back to his bed in nature.

Still he cannot sleep.

30.

It is early morning and Casey and Norman's night of sleeping together is complete. In spite of their troubles, each slept through the night but now they are being woken by endless knocking on Casey's door. More knocking. And more.

"I'm coming!" Casey is up and throws on jeans as the knocking continues. "Christ."

Norman opens his eyes and looks around, orientating himself to unfamiliar surroundings.

"How'd you sleep?" she asks him.

"Okay. I mean, I managed to get some sleep, yeah."

As she finishes dressing the knocking continues. He scrambles out of bed. "No rush," Casey tells him. "That'll be Philip. Best if you stayed put. He'll draw conclusions."

"I can handle Philip."

"Yeah only the theatrics are hard to take." She turns to go out the door.

"Hey," he says. "Today we find my family. Right?"

"Yes, we totally do."

She closes her bedroom door and says good morning to Vicious. She hollers out that she's coming and, arriving at the front door, leaves the chain on and peeks out at, yup, Philip.

"Good morning, Philip. And what exactly brings you here at such an early hour?"

"First, thank you for returning my car keys in the mail slot but it would have been nice had you dropped them off in person."

"It was late then and it's early now."

"Right. Moving on. To commence, I should rather cut my heart out with a pen knife than disturb you."

"How well put."

Vicious, next to Casey, growls. Philip asks who that might be. "It's a dog." Philip says he'd be happy to take it for a pee and Casey says she'll handle that herself. The less involved Philip is with their day, the better.

She keeps the chain on.

"I must speak with you," Philip begins. "I've been in anguish since yesterday at the diner. I'm afraid I'm having trouble concentrating on my work."

"Could we move this along?"

"I should like to apologize for my behavior. It was dreadful. There are no excuses."

"That's it? Great. Forgiven." She begins to close the door, his foot intervenes.

"I am completely and unreservedly sorry."

"As you said already. And as I said, you are forgiven. Now all you have to do is apologize for apologizing at such an ungodly time and we can both move on with our day."

"Of course. I apologize for that, too."

"I was joking. But thank you. Bye now." She starts to close the door and again he sticks his foot in. Vicious growls once more but he plunges on.

"Please. I have news. You'll be happy to hear it. I have quit the bottle. I'm a sober man. It has been very nearly three hours."

"I think it takes a little more time than that. Let's at least wait until you no longer smell like stale beer. But still, all the best with it. Goodbye again." She starts to close the door a third time but again he sticks his foot out; he asks if he can come in for a tea. She's tempted to give in but he's annoying and unpredictable.

"No time for that, not today." His foot remains where it is. "Philip, please."

Norman is there. "We should get going."

Philip stares through the opening in the door. "Oh I see. Yes indeed. It's confirmed then."

"We need to talk to Harvey," Norman is focused only on Casey. "And I was remembering how Jack seemed certain my parents were okay. I have a feeling he hasn't told us everything."

Casey realizes Norman is using the pronoun 'we', a development she is quietly excited about. She says, "So let's go." She turns to Philip. "Philip, move your foot and you might as well come in. However, we are leaving so no tea and no protracted apologies and no trouble." Philip removes his foot. "You have apologized quite enough." She undoes the latch and opens the door.

Philip does a little bow toward Casey as he walks by her but gives Norman a snarky look as he passes him. Vicious continues to emit low growls and stare at Philip. Philip ignores her.

"How nice for you two," he says. "I'm sure you'll be happy. But it's never Philip who gets to be happy, is it?"

"Cut the high-school drama and don't make assumptions," Casey says. "This is serious. Norman's brother and sister have been kidnapped and his parents are missing. We need to borrow your car again."

"You can't. I have errands. My electric toothbrush needs a battery and I'm low on socks."

"Philip, we are talking about children."

"Oh bloody hell. I'd apologize but you've forbidden me. That's dreadful news. Yes, by all means, take my car." He fishes his keys out of his pocket and hands them to her. "Perhaps I could come along? I might come in handy. Don't forget that I've quit the bottle."

"No, but thank-you," Norman says. "Here, have this." He hands Philip his bus ticket. "Refund it at the bus depot. Take the money and have a breakfast on me. I expect you could use some food and a coffee."

Philip makes a fuss about the ticket, even after Norman points out the reason he no longer needs it is because he, Philip, is lending them his car. Philip suggests they could become best friends and play soccer together ("we call it football back home") and go for sushi.

Casey, Norman and Vicious are out the door.

31.

Keeley sits in her room in her home nestled in woods near a golf course. She is finishing her oatmeal. Earl gives her a bowl in the morning – the cupboards are full of it – and he makes it without lumps. She hates admitting it but Earl's oatmeal is better than the oatmeal Norman makes. She feels guilty about liking oatmeal made by a horrible and mean stranger better than the oatmeal made by her own brother. She thinks it's probably not a good idea to confess her preference to Norman but she is in the habit of telling him everything and so likely will. If she ever sees him again.

A tear forms in each eye.

She wishes he was there to tell things to, like the story she overheard when the two young guys came back last night. It seems they again fired shots at a car her brothers were in – *Norman in a car*? – and then they found her brothers and a woman in Vancouver. *Norman in Vancouver*? She also heard them say they captured Riley but she finds that hard to believe because she hasn't heard his voice telling them he was going beat them up and stuff, which Riley surely would do. She figures the woman must be Casey, the detective who visited her shortly before the horrible people showed up. She liked Casey.

Keeley is relieved that, other than pushing pamphlets about the second coming in her slot and telling her the Lord works in mysterious ways, her captors have left her alone. The younger ones, one she calls The Son of Broom, the other one, Mister Nice-Guy, haven't been around much. When The Son of Broom is there he says mean things into the slot and she tells him to buzz off and calls him names. If no one else is inside the motor home, Mister Nice-Guy promises he'll take care of her. She told him that if he really meant it he would let her go "exactly right now" and if he does not then he is "just as horrible and mean and awful as the others."

Having finished her oatmeal, she goes to the slot her door and peers out. Mister Nice-Guy is guarding her, sitting in the chair by her door; he's fallen asleep. The others take walks in the woods twice daily to "speak with the Lord in his abundant home," or so she has heard them say; that is likely where they are now.

Peering through the door-slot, she notices Mister Nice-Guy's phone beside him on the arm of the chair and gets an idea. If she sticks her hand through the slot she can...almost...stretch and...her fingers are on it. She inches it closer. No! The phone hits a set of keys lying next to it, knocking the keys onto the floor. She quickly pulls her hand back. There's a snort from Mister Nice-Guy but he doesn't wake. Back out goes her hand –

She has the phone!

"I hate these things," she mutters as she examines Benjie's android. She is relieved to find no passcode. When she gets her own phone she is going to have a passcode, though mostly so Riley won't be able to use it. If, she thinks, *if* she ever gets away and *if* she even decides to have a phone one day.

She has operated friends phones so knows her way around them. Not much power left on this one. Her impulse is to dial the newspaper but she doesn't know the number by heart. She wants it to be Norman that rescues her, and Riley, so would prefer to call them instead of 911. But how can she get a hold of her brothers?

While Keeley was grabbing Benjie's phone, Casey and Norman were in Philip's Honda pulling up outside the office of the Current. For a change the drive was uneventful. Vicious spent it on

Norman's lap, occasionally licking his face. They sit outside the office and Norman asks Casey to give him a few moments with Jack. Everything his *Uncle* Jack knows, he wants to know.

He enters the office.

Jack is stacking bundles of the latest edition of the Current into a small wagon, the drop-off wagon, used to deliver papers around town. He looks up. "Harvey was just here," he says. "Told me about Riley and said if you showed up you should wait for him. I was just leaving to do some drop-offs."

"They can wait. We need to talk." Jack shrugs and sits at his desk. Norman stays standing. "I did my background work, like you said."

Jack holds up his hand. "I'll save you the trouble. You left a story on the computer so I know what this is about. You want to know why my brother James, and his wife, Lana, and myself, didn't tell you who I am."

"That, and other things."

"I am not practiced at talking about this."

"I figured some things out on my own. I gather my parents changed our surname and moved here to stay hidden from this Reverend Broom and Earl Porter."

"I changed my last name, too. I wanted distance and Hapgood is such a unique name. Your parents also considered changing their first names, and yours. If the internet was as advanced then as it is now they would have. How did these idiots find you anyhow?"

"The Telegraph picked up Riley's story and the photos."

"Really? I never read that paper."

"It's hard to accept two quasi-religious goons played such a role in shaping our lives."

"Everything changed after what they did. For me. For all of us. You know how I say Riley's boldness reminds me of somebody I grew up with? That somebody is your father. He was fearless. But all that changed after what they did. Then when Earl Porter's trial ended your father began getting notes in the mail. About how a wrong would be righted and he should prepare to have his family taken from this Earth. He was terrified for you and your mother. Obviously Broom was the number one suspect but other than the content of the notes he left no clues. But the notes convinced James and Lana to come up here. It was a measure of safety and he was able to practice his profession."

"Did you blame my father for what happened?"

"His stories exposed a false prophet. My brother did his job, and did it well. He just failed to see how insane Broom is and I lost my wife and son because of that."

"They got the wrong mother and son."

"Yes, our address was in the book, yours was not. They were too stupid to think two Hapgoods could be working at the same newspaper. For years, I hated you and your mother for being alive. I'm not proud of that."

"I can understand it."

"You know you owe your brother and sister's existence to Reverend Broom and Earl Porter." Norman doesn't look convinced. "If they hadn't attacked my family your parents would not have moved here and not long before the murders Lana told my wife she didn't plan on having more children. But living in a small town suited them and along came Riley and Keeley. So they got to live instead of my family so some gain came of it. Mind you, my wife wanted a dozen but we would've settled on five or so. They were all taken from me. Family was taken. I couldn't be with anyone else. I had to stop thinking about my loss so I took the easy route and started drinking. Yesterday was the first time

I saw a picture of my family since they were killed."

"I'm sorry about showing you that."

"You didn't know. Maybe it was time. Past time."

Norman let the silence settle then, tentatively: "What were their names?"

Jack puts his head in his hands and says nothing. Norman doesn't remember them but he would like to know who he lost. He also wonders if talking about them might be good for Jack. The silence sits.

At last his uncle raises his head. He sighs and looks upwards, as if he is trying to spot an image of them to show to his nephew.

"My wife, she was Patty Cox, Patty Hapgood. I called her Patty Cakes; a silly name from a nursery rhyme. I haven't said any of those names in so long. She was beautiful. Tall but nicely round. Such a bright mind, so alive. Never down, forever looking at life with a positive view. She loved being outdoors, always organizing hikes and trips to the beach. A teacher by trade and a wonderful mother by deed and a loving wife for every day of the four years we were together. I had a tendency to be dour – no surprise I guess – but she didn't mind. If I was in a mood, she'd say 'no problem, I'll do the laughing for the both of us.' And she would."

Jack gathers himself. "Our son was Cormac. Or just Mac. The Mac Man. The Mac Attack. Tough kid. Born five days after you; you came on the tenth, he came on the fifteenth. You would have been great friends. You already were. You didn't always share toys but not too many scrapes. Almost to the day Mac started walking he'd charge up to trees and kick them. It was like he wanted to knock them over. Kick 'em hard, too. Hurt his little feet but you'd have to pull him away. He'd be laughing. Yes. Laughing! Forever on the move. A lot like his cousin Riley in that regard. I'd be doing something in the kitchen and hear him pull things down from the living-room; I'd call out 'Hey somebody better get that guy.' This went on a few months and then Mac started using words. One day he knocked a vase onto the floor in there and from the kitchen I called out my usual 'Hey somebody better get that guy.' This time he answered: 'No, don't get that guy!' he said. His first sentence." He stops, composes himself. "The Mac Man died 23 days after his second birthday. That idiot Broom and his idiot henchman, they got that guy. They murdered my wife and son. Most of me died with them."

Norman lets a few tears drop. His Uncle looks as if in a trance and he can think of only tired words to offer, but he offers them all the same. "I'm so sorry for your loss," he tells Jack. "They sound wonderful, you had a wonderful family. They were my aunt and my cousin."

"They were indeed."

"I wish I could remember him," Norman says. "I think I do a little. I wish I could have grown up with them in my life. I will never stop wishing that."

"Thank you."

Norman slowly goes to Jack's chair and awkwardly lays his hand on his shoulder and leaves it there a moment. He walks to his desk and sits. He wipes his tears.

Jack says, "When I heard Earl Porter was released I started drinking even more. Lost another job. Your father found me, again, and offered work. The alcoholic knows that if he or she keeps drinking there are only three places you end up: in jail, in the psyche ward or in the grave. I wasn't ready for any of them so I said yes. His terms were I stop boozing; mine were that you kids were not to be told what happened or who I was. I didn't feel strong enough to get close."

"Do you know where my parents are, Uncle Jack?"

"Yes. I do know. I should have told you but you were in the dark about so much I didn't know how to get into it," he sees a flash of concern in Norman's eyes. "Don't get me wrong, they're fine. I waited on the highway for them and threw my javelin at their car, the same one from that picture of me and your father."

"You threw it at their car? Why?"

"I can't be sure. James told me about their camping plans and it caused the resentment to surface and I used it as an excuse to start back drinking and once I did that all bets were off. Didn't even aim but the javelin went through their windshield and they skidded into the lake. They got out though and swam to shore. I found them and they forgave me. Or my brother did, I'll have to work on my sister-in-law. Your father said a dip in the f'ing lake wasn't gonna stop them, his exact words. The storm was dying and the three of us collected up what supplies we could. Never found the javelin; I gather the police didn't either; let's hope it's down there forever."

"You could have killed them."

"Oh I know that. I suppose I intended to. When you're drunk you often know you're doing something wrong but you still do it. Bad excuse. Fact is, I love my brother. My wife loved him, too, she admired your father a great deal. Anyhow, your parents left to hike up the mountain and forever dispatch the fears they have of the past returning. Ironic hey? They should be back today."

He feels a weight has been lifted. He smiles up at his nephew. "So then. Moving forward. What about Riley and Keeley?"

"Broom has them. We don't know where."

"After living so long without emotions it feels strange to have them back," Jack stands and walks over to the drop-off wagon. "Maybe good even. Except now I'm full of fear for my nephew and niece. I'll get on with this but if there's anything I can do, just ask and I'll do it."

Picking up two bundles of newspapers from the counter, Jack

puts them on the wagon with the others already there and pulls the wagon out the door.

When Jack steps outside, Casey and Vicious are still in Philip's car. Casey watches Jack trudge along and turn a corner. Casey gets out of her car and is heading toward the Current's front door when her phone rings. She looks at the call display. Benjie Porter?

"Hello. Casey here."

A female voice. "Casey Collier, the detective?"

"That's me. Who is this?"

"You passed your business card under my door, which I am happy you did."

"Keeley? Hang on." Casey punches the Smart Voice app to record the call. "Keeley, still there? Are you okay?"

"No. I need you to take a message to my brother. Tell him I'm really, really *really* mad at him. You have to say it exactly like that."

"Wait. Don't hang up! He's right here." Casey rushes in the front door. Norman is at his desk, looking at maps of the area between Still Waters and Vancouver.

"It's Keeley!" she shouts. Norman looks up and she throws him the phone, a little high.

He snags it. "Keeley?"

"Norman? Norman *you promised*!"

"Oh God, I know. I'm so sorry."

"I borrowed this phone. I didn't even ask but they didn't ask to steal me."

"Keeley, are you okay?"

"No. Their oatmeal is good though."

"Great. Now where are you?"

"I'm in my room."

"Can you get out of it?"

"No, they put up locks."

"Tell me where your room is and I'll come get you."

"I don't know where. Last night I heard them say they had Riley, too. They said they can finish the job tomorrow but that means today because that was yesterday. Norman, what do you think 'finish the job' means?"

"I don't know but we'll get you out of there."

"They said Mom and Dad are gone and it means you're the head of our family and they want you to feel pain," she's crying. "Is our Mom and Dad gone?"

"No they are not gone. In fact Uncle Jack just told me a minute ago they're coming home today."

"Uncle Jack? We don't have an Uncle Jack."

"We do actually, but we can talk about that later. Now who said that stuff about tomorrow?"

"This Reverend guy said it to this fat Earl guy."

"Keeley, don't call people fat."

"He also said it to the Son of Broom, who is mean, and to Mister Nice-Guy, who I almost like because he talks nice but only when no one else is around. It's his phone I borrowed."

"I know them, I know who those two are."

"How come?"

"We can talk about that later, too. You're sure Broom said tomorrow?"

"He said everything had to be ready at noon tomorrow but that was yesterday he said that, so that means noon today. Norman, you have to hurry!"

"Okay, okay. Slow down. Now think carefully. Do you have any idea where they parked the motor home? Were there any clues?"

"No. Or wait. Yes. There was one," she picks up something from beside her laptop. "I think we might be near a ga – hey, no, I'm using it! Let me go you horrible..."

The phone is abruptly hung up.

"A ga? Keeley? Keeley?" He drops the phone on his desk and flops down into his chair.

Casey says, "What happened?"

"She's gone again."

32.

As Reverend Broom, Jerry and Earl Porter took a walk in the Lord's abundant home, the woods, they plotted strategy. As they had decided yesterday, the explosion would happen at precisely noon, a timer set so they could be on their way to the airport when their revenge (Reverend Broom called it their "divine retribution") was achieved. Jerry would set up a camera so Norman Hapgood, in their eyes now the head of the family after the presumed deaths of his parents, would later be able to see footage of his family disappearing forever.

It was time to set the plan in motion and leave for their flight. Returning from their walk, Earl, the explosives expert, begins to set up the detonator and timer outside the front door while Jerry begins mounting the camera on a tree across from the front door.

Reverend Broom goes inside to instruct Benjie to move Riley from the trunk of the Mercury into the bedroom where the siblings are to suffer their fate together. He finds Benjie sleeping and hears the voice of the girl whispering on a phone. He quietly unlocks each of the deadbolts and bursts into her room to find her on Benjie's cell. He grabs it and slaps her. She protests and kicks at him, missing. As he walks out she throws the golf ball she had in her hand at his back; it harmlessly strikes his jacket and falls to the floor.

He slams her door shut.

"I was talking with Justin Bieber," she yells. "And the Biebs is coming to get you. He cares about his fans!"

Reverend Broom does not know who Justin Bieber is but reasons it didn't matter who she was talking to, she could not give away their location because she doesn't know it. Could the police track it? They would be on their flight to Guyana before they could do that. In any case, he decides to have Jerry destroy the phone.

Benjie is woken by the commotion and finds himself next to an angry Reverend Broom engaging the deadbolts in Keeley's door. Finishing, he turns to Benjie.

"You've shown yourself to be a drought-bringer again," Broom bellows. "You are incurring God's wrath."

Benjie apologizes but knows the Reverend will take his revenge. The bellowing brings Jerry and Earl inside. "One punch shall be sufficient," Reverend Broom tells his son. "Try not to break any bones."

Jerry smiles broadly and begins to raise his fist. Benjie has the skills to stop him, and easily, but it isn't the time for that; not yet. He watches Jerry's fist coil back and fly forward. Smack in the face. Pain. He looks at his father standing there, making no move to help.

Jerry's injured right hand throbs but he ignores it. "Can I hit him again, Father?"

"Once is enough. Isn't that right, Benjie?" Benjie nods. "Back to your work, Jerry. You, too, Earl. We have a plane to catch." Jerry reluctantly goes outside.

Earl gets to the door and looks back to Benjie. "Son, you be a team player now, okay?" Earl goes out.

Reverend Broom says, "How did she get the phone? Did you give it to her?"

"No. I fell asleep. She must have reached through the slot to take it. You can't blame her though."

"I will blame whomever I see fit to blame."

"I only meant it was my fault."

"My son tells me you have become a reluctant member of our congregation. That you question, hesitate. You have taken your eyes from our goal, Benjie, and you're travelling down the wrong path. Consider your father and the loyalty you owe him."

"I do. I think about it all the time."

"And think of the rapture. The Bible says it will not come until savages have taken over this Earth. Everywhere we see that is the case. The date was never given, it's not for us to know. But savages rule and once I'm the supreme religious ruler of this temporal world the time will be upon us. Do you understand that?"

What Benjie understands is that the Reverend Broom talking about the savagery of others is hypocrisy. But he nods his head.

"I am returning now into God's abundant forest to pray for you. But I advise you to think about this." Broom is at the door. "God has been good to you. You must worship him in return. You must worship me." The self-titled Reverend Broom goes out the door.

"That guy is horrible," Keeley says, peering out the slot.

Benjie says, "Yes. I think you're right about that."

"Are you okay? I have some headache tablets."

"I'm okay, but thank you."

"Sorry about getting you in trouble."

"It wasn't your fault, Keeley."

"How'd you know my name?"

"You've been on the news. I'm Benjie."

"Are you gonna let me go, Benjie?"

"I hope and pray that's what happens but I don't know how this will end. I wish I did."

"Please, I just want my family back. I'm scared."

"I promise I won't abandon you. I have to go."

Benjie makes his way out the door and down the stairs. Thirty feet away, Jerry stands making adjustments to a mount he is securing to the tree. A video camera sits on the ground nearby.

Meanwhile, to Benjie's right Earl is kneeling down off to the side of the front entrance, placing wires. Benjie watches as his father finishes hooking three wires up to the detonator and begins unspooling two more.

"Dad, what is that black thing, exactly?"

"That is the detonator and that is a timer," his father replies, pointing to each. "I'm using five wires."

"To set off explosives?"

"These three are to confuse any do-gooder who might try to defuse it. These last two, one disarms the device if needed, the other fires the explosives. This is the fun part, devising an explosion in my own way. I get to make it up, much like creating your own puzzle."

"You're not creating. You're destroying."

Jerry overhears this. "That is blasphemy," he says. Moving quickly to Benjie, he grabs him by the collar and raises him up. "Do you want me to hit you again?"

Earl says, "Jerry. Come on. You've made your point. Let it alone." Earl jams his arm between the two. "I'll talk to my son."

Jerry releases him. "You better talk to him good." He goes back to mounting the camera while Earl hustles Benjie around to the side of the motor home.

"What is this about?" he demands.

"Those kids are innocent," Benjie says.

"Do you not feel the pain of our lost congregation?"

"They had nothing to do with it."

"In his wisdom, the Reverend knows these children won't be included in the rapture anyhow."

"You can't know that. When you were in prison I enjoyed the gatherings, the other children, being a part of something. I liked Reverend Broom. But why must there be this obsession with revenge and destruction? There's no purpose to it."

"It is a part of our preparation to be lifted."

"I read those stories. Their father was right about the greed and the hypocrisy. Look how he lived, and how others lived while giving him their money and possessions. Like my mother and I."

A voice comes from around the corner: "So you believe those stories?" Reverend Broom steps out and stands before them. "Instead of me or your father. Instead of believing our Savior, you accept the blasphemy."

"He didn't mean that, Reverend."

"Shut up, Earl. Tell us, Benjie."

"I believe you were living an opulent lifestyle while others lived with far less. Some with very little."

"That is because I am their guiding light."

"I grew up without a father because he paid for two murders he did not commit. And now you're trying to get him to kill innocent children?"

"And how do you know that, Benjie? How do you know he did not commit those murders?"

Earl says, "Reverend, please. Not now."

"No. I think it is finally time. He needs to know." Reverend Broom stares at Benjie. "So, Benjie? How do you know your father did not commit those killings?"

"Because he told me. Because my mother believed in him. And because I read the transcripts of his trial. You testified on his behalf. You said Bud Clement killed them and he acted alone. He killed them and went into hiding and has never been found."

"I'm afraid what Bud Clement was guilty of was fornicating with my wife. The sinful Bud Clement has not been found since because he is buried in cement in front of my former home. It was my ex-wife who escaped to the U.S.. Bud Clement was not so lucky."

Benjie is stunned. Did his father have anything to do with all this killing? "I get it now," Benjie says. "'Buried in cement, just like Clement.' But who killed him, who killed Bud Clement?"

Reverend Broom looks to Earl. "Shall I tell him, Earl, or will you?"

"You don't need to," Benjie says. "I get the picture." He looks to his father. "So then it was also you that killed that woman and her two-year-old son?"

Earl says, "We were protecting our ministry. Doing God's work. They wouldn't have been lifted up."

"You passed judgement on a two-year-old?"

Reverend Broom says, "I did. It was my need for revenge that fueled it and gave it meaning. I planned the explosion, your father carried it out. It was regretful we got the wrong family but understandable given the circumstances; brothers at the same newspaper with sons the same age. The Lord must have wanted it so. Your father is right, they were not worthy of being lifted up to the heavens, they were not true adherents and would have been left here to suffer. Make no mistake, being a true Christian is the standard and I can help you reach it."

Benjie is focused only on his father. "You did this because he told you to? You did it for revenge?"

"Don't think it unimportant, son. It's necessary to avenge and in protecting a ministry of God we were performing a Holy act." Earl recites, "*It is mine to avenge. I will repay. In due time their foot will slip; their day of disaster is near and their doom rushes upon them.*"

"Nicely chosen, Earl."

"I won't be a part of this anymore," Benjie says. "I won't take part in deciding who God loves and who He leaves behind. And I won't be a part of killing anyone. I'm leaving the ministry."

Earl says, "But you gave your word. You promised your mother you would obey."

"It was based on a lie. She wouldn't want this. She wouldn't know who you are." Benjie is backing away from hs father.

Jerry is behind him, pointing his gun at the back of his head. "This time, I do it," he says.

There's no need for Benjie to hold back anymore. He's fast and Jerry doesn't respect the martial arts and has little idea of what it can do. He certainly does not expect the skill Benjie has. Twisting, Benjie's right hand chops the gun to the ground as his left jabs Jerry in the stomach, knocking the air out of him. A swift kick to the side of a knee and then he punches Jerry in the mouth once, twice – Smack! Smack! – and grabs him by the shoulders, shoving him forward and face-first into the dirt, kneeling and jamming his knee onto to his back. Grabbing the younger Broom's arm and wrenching it behind his back, he warns Jerry if he moves he'll break it.

Benjie picks up the gun and straightens up, placing a foot on

Jerry's back, keeping him pinned down.

He looks up to see his father pointing a gun at him.

Reverend Broom: "Go ahead, Earl. Send him to hell."

Earl freezes.

Benjie says, "She was at your trial every day. Visited you every week, even when she became ill. What would she say if she could see who you really are?"

"Who I am, son? I am a man of God. And I do his bidding through Reverend Broom. I will be raptured. I will be lifted up to her."

"She wouldn't have you."

There is a silence and then Reverend Broom's voice: "Shoot him I said!"

Earl shakes his head and slowly lowers his gun. "If you don't want to be a part of our ministry, go. If you change your mind, I'll be in Guyana." He turns to the Reverend. "You owe me this." Reverend Broom nods.

Benjie backs up a step and another and another and then he turns and runs into the trees.

As soon as he's out of sight, Jerry, in pain, starts to hoist himself but falls back down. From the ground he motions for Earl's gun but his father shakes his head.

"I can catch him," Jerry pleads.

The Reverend says, "I'm not so sure you are capable of bettering him. In any case, we shall go to Guyana without young Benjie Porter. But don't be mistaken: God will see to him. We have our revenge to take."

In the woods, Benjie keeps running.

33.

Things were unravelling for Philip Briggs and after Norman and Casey left he sat brooding on Casey's two-seater couch. His work, communicating with co-workers in England and conducted from his living-room, has lost its meaning. Why should he care about renewable energy and carbon services when the woman he loved was dating a longish-haired sensitive type? The kind of man most women enjoyed nowadays.

"And what about you, lad," Philip said to himself. "You are a brute; your only interests are the bottle, football and chips. You don't have a single sensitive bone. No wonder he's been chosen over you."

Losing was becoming tiresome.

Philip may have sat despondent for days had not something unexpected happened. He was thinking deeply about the patterns of his behavior and he had this: an epiphany. His first ever.

It happened suddenly, which is what epiphanies do. He was sure that's what he'd had and sure the clarity it gave to him would help rid him of his despondency and change his life for the better. However, to be certain he rushed down the hall to his own apartment and looked it up online. Under epiphany at dictionary.com this is what he found:

A sudden, intuitive perception of, or insight into, the reality or the essential meaning of something, usually initiated by some...commonplace occurrence or experience...a moment of revelation and insight.

Yes! That was precisely what he'd had! For starters, through *in-*

tuitive perception he suddenly realized he 'd done the following three things: 1) he had meekly apologized to Casey; 2) he acted like a wimp when it was confirmed she had a new lover; and 3) he fawned over Norman for giving him a bus ticket when, thanks to him, the man no longer needed it anyhow.

Upon examining these behaviors Philip became aware the *commonplace occurrence* that lead to his epiphany was actually all three combined. In a *moment of revelation* he realized they were commonplace *occurrences*, plural, part of a pattern that saw him forever playing the lower status role of an underling, of a weak and irresolute man.

It came to him that raising his status in their eyes was a key to raising it *in his own eyes*. That would free him of the crippling sorrow he encountered upon being spurned; indeed it would help him to overcome the perverse need he had of being spurned in the first place.

Raising his status, that was the key.

"Hooray!" said Philip, out loud. "I bleeding well got it at last." He then exhorted himself, again out loud, to take his place in the world. "Take your bloody place on this planet, Philip!" he shouted. "'Ya stupid git."

This is the plan he devised: he'd use the bus ticket to Still Waters and upon his arrival there provide Casey and her lover – yes, lover, that was all well and good with him now – the solution to their problem (whatever it was; he'd paid no attention but would figure it out later).

They would then have no choice but to view him as someone who had the talent and forthrightness to achieve goals. Someone who did not allow a minor thing such as being cast aside to affect his happiness and impair his relationship with the world around him. This view would replace their current viewing of him as a supplicant, a child, a wounded puppy.

And there was the reason for this effort: for with their respect and admiration he would, in turn, be able to change the manner in which he viewed himself.

Freedom!

He resolved he would go through the logic again during the bus ride to Still Waters. Once on the bus, he began by enjoying the trip, travelling through areas he'd never seen, for mostly all Philip had seen of Canada was his apartment, Casey's apartment (a mirror image of his), the diner across the street, a nine-hole public golf course and a multitude of drinking establishments.

But alas, things did not continue smoothly. As the bus wound its way along the Tran-Canada Highway, his penchant for self-doubt began to prey upon him as he went over again the meaning of his epiphany. It was becoming unclear. Further, how could he provide a solution to a problem when he didn't know what the problem was? He doubted it was an I.T. problem, the only kind of problem he could be certain of solving.

He became so full of wretched thoughts about failure that when the bus pulled off the highway for a brief stop at a suburban mall, he vaulted inside to a liquor store and purchased a bottle of his favorite whisky.

To help remain resolute.

By the time he arrived in Still Waters he'd enjoyed a good portion of the bottle and his hiccupping had made an enemy of the fellow next to him. Along the way he lost all belief in his "illogical and insane" epiphany – for that is how he referred to it now – and admonished himself for devising such an absurd plan.

So it was that instead of arriving at the Still Waters B S Depot – he was mildly amused by the sign – in a state of mental vigor, he arrived in a timorous mood.

Nonetheless he was determined to succeed and asked directions to the newspaper and soon found himself outside of its front entrance. He took another drink, one more and another still. By this time, he was, as they say in England, barking up a tree.

In he went.

34.

In the newspaper office Casey, Norman and Harvey are crowded around Norman's desk about to listen to the recording of Keeley's call. Vicious lays nearby. It is turning into the hottest day of the year and the heat and the worry are beginning to take a toll.

Harvey has asked to hear the part of the conversation, the end of it, in which Keeley is cut off; Casey is about to play it when Philip walks through the door. Vicious growls softly as Norman looks up and grimaces.

"Look who's here," he says.

Casey says, "Philip, how the hell did you get here?"

"I used the bus ticket. And again I thank you, Norman. No. Never mind. I take that back." He regroups mentally, telling himself *don't be a wimp*.

"We don't' have time for this," Casey says. "This is serious."

"Who is this man?" Harvey asks.

"My neighbour," Casey says. "He's from England."

Philip tries out his plan to raise his status: "No disparaging my country. We gave the world The Beatles and the Magna bleeding Carta. Not to mention Shakespeare and more pubs than you could visit in a dozen lifetimes."

Casey says, "How very nice. Now please - "

"And the Royal Family and Abba. No. Not Abba. That wasn't us.

The Spice Girls. Oh hey - and Tom Hardy; brilliant actor."

Casey says, "What happened to sobriety?"

"Sober as a British magistrate on vacation." He hops onto the front counter, with his bottle. "I promise if I've nothing to offer then I shall offer nothing."

Harvey says, "And I promise if you keep interrupting I'll arrest you for obstruction of justice."

"Right. I'll shut up."

Harvey nods at Casey and she hits the app on her phone, holding it up for the others to hear. It starts in the middle of Keeley and Norman's conversation:

"I know who those two are."

"How come?"

"We can talk about that later, too. You're sure Broom said tomorrow?"

"Yes. He said everything had to be ready at noon tomorrow but that was yesterday he said that, so that means noon today. Norman, you have to hurry!"

"Okay, okay. Slow down. Now think carefully. Do you have any idea where they parked the motor home? Were there any clues?"

"No. Or wait. Yes. There was one. I think we might be near a ga – hey, no, I'm using it! Let me go you horrible – "

Casey stops it.

Norman says, "It has to be a gas station."

"I agree," Harvey says. He looks at his watch. "It's almost ten-thirty. That only gives us ninety minutes. I'll radio the chopper and have cars check around every gas station between here and the city."

"There's something else," Casey says. "Riley found a pamphlet on explosives at the house."

"No surprise there. I'll get the demo guys on standby."

Casey says, "But what if a gas station wasn't what she was trying to say?"

Norman says, "The word obviously started with a 'g' and it was followed by an 'a'. Gas station is all there is."

Philip says, "Perhaps a ga-alaxy?"

Casey says, "Philip, you've been warned."

"I agree with Norman," Harvey says. "It's a gas station. Now last night didn't go well so stay put and I'll keep you updated. Let us do our job."

Harvey is out the door.

Casey watches Harvey walk past the window, he's already on the phone making arrangements. Authority never impressed her. Ask her parents. In many ways though Harvey does meet her standards, he's not heavy-handed and he listens well enough. But trying to prevent her from finding Keeley and Riley, to stop her from getting closer to Norman and his family, that doesn't meet with her approval.

"He can't tell you what to do," she suddenly says, turning to Norman.

"Here we go again," Norman says.

"All I'm saying is we have a right to look. And there's not much time so the more hands on deck, the better." She grabs a notepad and pen.

"But we don't have anywhere to look," Norman tells her. "He said they'd cover the gas stations and that's where they are: near a gas station."

Here's this: Norman doesn't want to entertain the idea of his home being anywhere else because if it's anywhere else the odds of finding it in time are not so good. But hidden in woods behind a gas station near the highway, that would have been a logical choice and a well-coordinated police search will find it. So in his mind it's near a gas station.

Period.

Casey, however, she isn't convinced. On the notepad, she writes a 'g' and an 'a' but other than 'gas station' all she can think of is 'garage.'

"Could it be near a garage?" she asks. "Maybe like a parking garage somewhere?"

"There would have been sightings."

"If there were such a thing as an actual 'ga'," Philip pipes up. "That would solve everything."

Casey says, "Philip, please."

"I suggest free association," Philip keeps going. "Which I excel at: gallant, gambit, gate, galley. Oh, say, what about being near a ga-argoyle? Seems possible."

"Enough," Casey says. "In fact, please leave. Out. I mean it. Go." She points to the door. Philip is somewhat taken aback. He's being banished? "Philip – goodbye."

"What? You're really saying I should get lost?"

"We're trying to find Keeley and Riley and you're free associating nonsense. So yes, get lost. Now."

"Bloody hell. Fine then." Philip is stung. "Out I go into the great beyond." He's at the door but stops. "Oh, wait, I shall require the keys to my vehicle."

"You're drunk," Casey tells him. "You can't drive."

"I should only like them to fetch my golf clubs from the trunk;

won't get behind the wheel, scouts honor."

"You mean that?" He vigorously nods his head. "Because we don't need any more drama." He again vigorously nods his head. She throws him his keys.

Philip gone, Casey looks up gas stations on the route into Vancouver. Google Map includes photos and Casey argues none have areas around them where a mobile home could be hidden.

Norman is fairly certain the family's motor home could not traverse bumpy rural roads and so must be near the highway; he points out two gas stations that are a possibility, though in truth he can't be sure.

The office is scorching hot now and Casey goes to the front counter to turn on the fan. The front door opens and in comes Jack Smith; he has a bottle, carrying it openly now. Walking past Casey, he sits at his desk.

"There's a guy drinking whisky out there." he says. "Hitting golf balls into Bluewater Park."

"That would be Philip. He's a friend of Casey's."

"Have they found them?" Jack asks.

"No," Norman says. "Harvey has about 90 minutes to locate the motor home and disarm the explosives. Keeley and Riley are inside. It's near a gas station between here and Vancouver but we don't know which one."

"So you're waiting to hear?"

"That's the plan Norman came up with," Casey says, turning on the fan and moving toward Jack. "But I think we should do something besides sit around in this heat looking mournful."

Norman says, "Harvey knows what he's doing."

"Sure. But consider this: what if it's not a gas station?"

"But it is."

"Norman, your brother and sister need you and you've regressed back to being a catatonic."

"We did something. Remember? Yesterday. We made it worse."

"So this time we'll make it better."

"Why are you still even here?" Norman says.

"What do you mean by that?"

"I mean you're not a part of this family. You're not even a detective. You quit, remember? That's your thing, isn't it? Afraid to finish things so you quit."

"Oh and you've got such a great track record." she fires back. "Two days ago you'd never ridden on a bus or been to a city; you couldn't even cross a street without making a Broadway production out of it."

"And you're a telemarketer whose parents ran away on her."

Ouch. That hurts. It sits for a moment. Casey shakes her head. She's not wanted, that's clear to her now.

"I guess my first impression of you was the right one," she finally says. "You are a coward." She picks up Vicious. "I hope they're found safe."

On her way out the door she turns off the fan. "Sorry Jack," she says. "But I want him to feel the heat."

35.

The countryside Benjie walks in is quiet, calm. Sun beaming brilliantly, birds flitting from tree to tree, there's lots of green and he's trying to use his love of nature to distract himself from what just happened.

He came out of the woods two lengths of a football field from the motor home and is walking along the side of a rural, unpaved road, the road his father drove over on the way to the clearing. He has the gun he took from Jerry; he considered throwing it away but in the end tucked into the back of his pants. He's not sure what to do with it but he never intends to fire it again.

There is this though: despite believing violence is not a legitimate problem solving tool he got pleasure from besting Jerry. He has a slight bruise on his cheek from where Jerry hit him in the motor home but he knows it's nothing compared to the injuries he inflicted upon Jerry. It wasn't hard, either, not for him; with his training it was an unfair fight.

Oh well, he thought, allowing a slight smile.

Estranged, that's the word Benjie feels describes his new relationship with his father, or lack of relationship. All those years of waiting for his release, believing him innocent, now meaningless. As a boy, going to the courthouse with his mother while she proclaimed her husband's innocence to the media and anyone who would listen, those experiences, too, meaningless. It leaves a sour taste.

But here's this: he still feels a strong pull toward the man. Too many years of yearning for a father, for his father, to simply let go.

It will take time.

If what his father did in the past wasn't reason enough to let go, there are two compelling reasons in the present: the girl and her brother. No amount of believing in the rapture could justify harming them and the more distance between himself and the children the more guilt he feels about leaving them behind.

He thinks how it would have broken his mother's heart to learn her husband really did commit murder. It would be even harder for her to learn her son walked away while Earl Porter killed again. Walked away after promising two children he would help them.

It becomes difficult for Benjie to put one foot forward in front of the other.

36.

Norman is wallowing in a fear born of hopelessness and there is no one to help him find a measure of optimism. Jack is drunk and Casey left ten minutes ago. Worse, he's heard nothing from Harvey.

He sits sweating in the heat.

The owner of the local barber shop, Sandie Birch, walks in with an ad. She's really come to find out about a rumor. The town knows of Keeley but now there's talk that Riley is missing. Earlier this morning a local was paying a fine at the RCMP office and he claims he overheard that Riley had been kidnapped, too.

She looks around the office. No Riley. "I hope I'm not being nosey," she says to Norman, "but has Keeley been found? And what about Riley?"

Norman is uncharacteristically brusque. "Well, you are being nosey," he says. "But for the record things don't look very good just now."

Sandie slinks out without placing an ad.

When the door closes behind her, Jack takes a swig of his bottle, stands and walks over to Norman, whose head has flopped down upon his desktop.

"Sit up and listen to me. Come on. Up." Norman slowly raises his head. "Sit right on up, pay close attention." Norman straightens but doesn't look at his uncle.

"Patty and Mac were gone before I knew anything was wrong,"

Jack says. "Two cops in suits walked up to my desk, like I just walked up to yours, and in seconds my life changed forever. It was over that quickly."

Now Norman looks at him.

"I would have grabbed on to even a remote chance of changing that outcome. There was none. I can't tell you what to do but you best be sure you can live with sitting here on your rear end while there's still a chance to save them. They sure as hell deserve better."

Jack returns to his bottle.

Outside the office, Sandie Birch wonders who the man hitting golf balls into Bluewater Park is. She'd like to tell him to stop but wants to tell her husband about her encounter with Norman. Besides, the man seems drunk and now he's leering at her and smiling. Weird.

Sandie rushes off.

Having failed to solve Casey and Norman's problem, Philip returned to being lovesick. He decided to employ physical exercise as a balm to salve his emotional wounds and is launching tee shots across the street onto the Bluewater soccer field. There was a woman watching him and he gave her his best smile but she ran off. Oh well. He wallops a ball that hits the door of the building that houses the change rooms. Looking about to make certain no one saw, Philip places another ball on a tuft of roadside grass.

Norman comes out of the Current office on his way to find Casey and look for his family. Where? He doesn't know. Anywhere. Jack was right. He has to try.

Philip bounces the next ball off the front of the 'Bluewater Park' sign across the street. It caroms back in the direction of the newspaper office, landing on the road and rolling to a stop at Norman's feet.

"That would be mine," Philip says, then hiccups.

Norman picks the golf ball up and flips it to him. "Shouldn't hit balls into the park," Norman says, turning to rush off. "Not that I care."

"Yes, well I thought a round of ga" – Philip hiccups again – "...olf might be invigorating."

Norman stops, turns, stares at Philip, a quizzical look upon his face. "What word did you just say?"

"I believe I said a few words. Invigorating?"

"You said something about golf."

"Yes, I did indeed. I said a round of golf."

"Say it again."

"Why? What are you up to?"

"Please. Just say the word golf again. Wait." Norman raises his hand to Philip's mouth and angles it sideways with his palm facing Philip. "Say golf now. SAY IT!"

"A...a round of golf." Norman slaps his hand over Philip's mouth, too late.

"Hey!" Philip says. "On guard, you blackguard."

"It's okay. There's nothing to worry about. Trust me, please. You're being extremely helpful."

"How am I being helpful by allowing you to smack me in the face?"

"You're helping me to solve the biggest problem I've had in the entirety of my life."

"I am?"

"You are. Now please say golf again. But wait a sec." Norman poises his hand over Philip's mouth. Not surprisingly, Philip is suspicious but he rather likes the idea of helping to solve Norman's problem. After all, with the goal of raising his status he came here to do just that.

"Okay," Norman says. "Go ahead: say golf."

"Right. Let's do this. A round of ga..." Norman jams his hand over Philip's mouth at just the right time.

"Yes! That's it!" Norman shouts. "Perfect. You did it!"

"I did? What precisely did I do?"

"You figured out where my brother and sister are."

"I did? *I* did that?" Philip bellows. "I came to do it and I bleeding well did it!"

"Quick, which way did Casey go?"

"Another problem? I'll solve this one too: my neighbour, and your lover, and that nasty little dog she's taken a shine to, went 'round that corner there," he points. "She seemed rather displeased."

Norman runs off, yelling back at Philip to follow in the car. Turning the corner, he spots Casey and Vicious, side by side, sitting upon a park bench on the other side of the street.

"Casey, hey, hi, stay there!"

She gets up and walks in the opposite direction.

Norman bolts into the middle of traffic, turns, faces an oncoming car and raises his hands, palms out. "Stop!" he shouts. The car jolts to a stop. It's Agnes and Margaret. Norman gives them the thumbs up and dashes into the next lane of traffic. A bus is heading at him. He again thrusts out his hands and the driver stops.

Norman runs across to the sidewalk.

Casey watched all this, stunned. Here he is before her, panting.

"You were right," he tells her. "They're not at a gas station. Even if the next letter isn't an 'a' some words beginning with a 'g' have a ga sound."

"Really? So you're a linguist now?"

"They're at the golf course. Ga-olf. No time to demonstrate but it makes sense. My father did a story on a back road out that way that connects with the golf course. The turn-off is the intersection those idiots keep waiting at."

"Great. So tell Harvey."

"If you want something done in this world, you do it yourself, right?"

"If you believe that sort of thing."

"I do."

"You don't need me. I'm just a telemarketer, remember? My parents dumped me."

"I'm truly sorry I said those things." Philip pulls up in the Honda. Norman says, "I gotta go. They need me. I think they need you, too."

Norman walks to the driver's side. "You're drunk," he says to Philip. "Shove over." Philip moves over.

Not only has Norman never driven but it's a standard. Philip tells him to put it in gear and push in the clutch with his left foot, then let it out while applying gas with his right. Norman stalls it. He restarts it.

And stalls it again.

On the sidewalk, Vicious sits watching the Honda. He whimpers. Casey looks over to the car.

Stall/start, stall/start.

Casey sighs. She wants to go. She wants to find Keeley and Riley. To help Norman. To finish something. To be part of a whole.

Stall/start, stall/start.

Vicious barks.

"Oh what the hell."

Casey walks to the driver's door. Norman reaches over and opens the passenger door, shoves Philip along, Philip spills out onto the pavement.

"Hey, it's my bloody car!"

"In the back," Norman orders. "Quick."

In he goes, Vicious scrambling in next to him. He smiles at her. She growls.

Casey jams it in gear and pulls into the road. As they careen through town Norman and Philip demonstrate the theory on 'ga' meaning 'golf;' Norman smacks Philip in the face - "ga!" - and Casey is convinced.

She steps on the gas.

As they drive out of the city they encounter a traffic jam so she runs up on the sidewalk, around the line-up of cars, into a crosswalk and then zooms through a red light. It's all done without anyone being hurt, though she did scrape a mailbox. Norman takes it very well.

"No harm, no foul," he says.

Onto the highway they drive alongside of the lake. They pass a newly erected 'You Are Now Leaving Still Waters' sign. Casey ignores the creaks and bangs and has the Honda doing over 130.

"Shit. I forgot. My phone is dead," she says. "Do you have yours, Philip?" He doesn't. Lost. Hasn't seen it in days. Casey says, "I should have called Harvey."

"I'd say we got this covered on our own," Norman tells her. "Hey, turn here!" He points.

Casey turns onto the gravel road at the intersection Jerry and Benjie waited at. They bounce and jostle and the Honda threatens to fall apart.

At a fork in the road she stops. On the left is one unpaved road, on the right is another, this one with a sign that reads: 'Road Closed: Flooding.'

"Don't forget the advice someone once gave," Philip says. "'If you come to a fork in the road, take it.'"

"Again, Philip, you fail to grasp the gravity of the situation," Casey says.

"Yes, well, I'm the bloke who figured out where they are."

Casey looks to Norman. "They wouldn't take a motor home down a washed out road. It must be left." She starts to go to the left.

"Wait," Norman says. Casey stops. "This area's being cleared for a hydro project; I followed the hearings for the paper. It was chosen because of its elevation. It's too high, couldn't flood."

"So why the sign?"

"I've never seen a sign like that around here. It's not a municipality sign." Norman starts to get out to move the sign but Casey grabs his shoulder. "No time." She guns it through the barrier.

Along the side of the road ahead walks Benjie. He told the children he would be there for them and he's going back to keep his promise. If he can't disarm the explosives he'll suffer the same fate; he hopes by doing so his mother in heaven will be able to forgive him.

He hears a car and slips back into the woods. Crouched in bushes, he realizes it's coming from the direction of town so it couldn't be the Mercury that Jerry stole. He can see it now, it's the rust-red Honda.

Now he hears the Mercury coming from the other direction. He begins to worry Reverend Broom will have Jerry and his father shoot at the Honda to prevent it from reaching the rigged motor home.

His hand grips the gun. Could he shoot his father to save those children? He watches as the cars draw closer.

Inside the Honda, they see an older model Mercury in the distance and figure it must be Broom.

Inside of the Mercury, Jerry spots the familiar rust-red Honda and tells his father it's the other brother. Reverend Broom realizes the girl somehow knew where they were and told her brother over the phone.

"Why would he attempt to rescue his family on his own without calling the police?" he asks his son.

"That's how dumb they are," Jerry tells him. "Him and that woman think they're detectives or something"

"That is fortunate for us. We can't let them get to the motor home. Block the road. We'll decide what to do with them later."

Jerry slams on his brakes and cranks the wheel to the right, spins sideways and stops. His side of the car is facing the oncoming Honda. He pulls out his gun. In the backseat, Earl does the same.

"Shit," Casey says. "It's them all right."

She slams on her brakes and cranks her wheel to the right and she, too, comes to a stop sideways, with her side of the car facing the Mercury.

Twenty yards apart, there's no other traffic and the woods on either side of the road give the unfolding drama a sense of isolation.

Silence as Reverend Broom, Jerry and Earl in the Mercury, and Casey, Norman and Philip in the Honda, stare across at one another.

Casey says, "They're just looking at us."

"It's creepy," Philip says.

"Keeley and Riley must be in the motor home," Casey says. "We have twenty-five minutes until noon so we need to get past them and fast."

"Sure," Norman says. "Only how do we do that?"

Reverend Broom is working out his plan of action: "If we simply remain here they won't be able to get past us to the motor home."

Earl says, "But we'll miss our flight."

Reverend Broom says, "Indeed we will."

"And if we go," Jerry is thinking hard as he speaks. "Then...they might be able to stop the explosion."

"Exactly," the Reverend says

"So what then?" Jerry asks his father.

"So start shooting, that's what."

"Yes!" Jerry does a fist pump.

In the Honda, Philip is squinting his eyes and trying to get a bead on what's going on in the other car. "Hey," he says. "The guy in the front and yeah, the one in the back, it looks like they both stuck guns out their windows. Might that be possible?"

"It certainly is," Casey yells. "Out."

Casey slides over and follows Norman out the passenger side, pulling her shoulder bag with her. Vicious scrambles into the front and jumps out behind Casey.

Philip stays in the back seat feeling around the floor for what's left of his whisky. Finding it, he pulls off the lid and raises it to his lip and - BLAM! the bottle shatters.

Shots are ringing out.

"God, who are these wankers?" He is out the door and throws himself to the ground.

The shooting stops. Casey pulls the gun she got at the former Broom mansion out of her shoulder bag. Standing, she fires wildly twice and drops back down.

Vicious has heard enough and runs off into the woods.

"I don't like this," Philip says.

"Neither do I," Casey says. "And we don't have time for it. I'm not likely to hit anyone, let alone three anyones. I don't think we have any choice but to negotiate."

"We don't have anything to offer." Norman peeks over the hood of the Honda. "They're getting out."

At the Mercury, the Brooms and Earl are spilling out and getting in behind the car.

"I would not have thought they would have a gun," Reverend Broom says.

"It's one of mine," Jerry says. "She got it at the house."

Reverend Broom says nothing about Jerry losing his gun. "Just deal with them quickly," is what he mutters.

Jerry inches upward, sticks his gun out and fires twice. Earl fires. Casey returns fire, two shots.

Now a voice.

"Broom?" Norman is calling out. "Broom, my brother and sister are innocent in all this."

"Would that be Mister Miller I hear?" Reverend Broom yells. "Or I should say Mister Hapgood. Norman Hapgood. Such a wonderful name, a pity your family decided to let it go."

"We were forced to. By a murderer."

"By a man deserving of respect," the Reverend yells. "Which your father refused to give to me. I think it unfortunate he is gone, however, but only because he won't see this."

Norman leans his head back against the Honda and looks up to the clear blue sky. How can he reach this man? He doesn't think logic will do it.

Begging?

"Look, you deserved better." Norman winces saying it. "I apologize for the actions of my father. I'm sorry for the stories he wrote. How is that? I could put it in writing. Please let them go. It was a long time ago."

"A long time ago? I still feel the repercussions," Broom is angry now. "My ministry destroyed. Legions of adherents who needed to be prepared for the lifting left without guidance because James Hapgood told them lies."

"Okay, I understand that. But you've disrupted our lives and taken our home. Isn't that enough revenge? They're children."

"Retribution, Mister Hapgood, is the divine right of Kings," Broom yells. "And I, in my own humble fashion, am King-like. I determine life and death and I am sending them to hell."

He nods at Jerry and Earl. "Shoot them. We have a plane to catch and I'd like to get out of this heat."

The two stand and start firing.

Casey, Norman and Philip throw themselves to the ground and cover their ears as a barrage of bullets shatter the car's windows, ping off of the frame and ricochet off rocks and gravel. The shooting stops.

Casey stands and fires two shots.

Jerry and Earl get back down behind their car to reload, each taking out another cartridge.

Philip crawls into the Honda's back seat looking for a piece of bottle that may still hold a drop of alcohol. No such luck but his hand feels something under the seat.

It's his lost cell phone.

"Remember I said I lost my phone? Found it. Must have dropped it while vacuuming back there. Be nice to die without having to worry about that."

Casey says, "Is it charged?"

"Works like a stevedore."

"Give." She grabs the phone and passes it to Norman. "Call Harvey."

"Shouldn't we just get in the car and go?"

"No way we'd get past them." As Norman dials she peeks over the hood. "Broom?" she calls. "We're calling the police. It'll be a lot worse for you if you don't let us get to them."

Earl promised himself no more jail time. "We really have to go, Reverend."

Jerry says, "She's used all the bullets in that gun. I'm almost certain. I can easily finish them off."

"Then go, shoot them; and be quick about it."

Jerry is out from behind the car, gun drawn; he walks purposely toward the Honda. One knee cracked and two ribs broken from Benjie's beating, his gait is part Zombie, part Hunchback of Notre Dame.

Norman hangs up; Harvey is on the way.

"Shit. Look at him. He's like a fricking monster." Casey calls out to Jerry. "You're an easy target. I'll shoot."

"This time it's you that has the empty gun," Jerry says, slowly, steadily advancing. "I kept track."

"Jesus, for someone so stupid he might be pretty smart." Casey tries to open the gun. "Anyone know how to tell if it's empty?" Two blank stares. "Great."

She leans over to see around the hood; Jerry lurched to his left and sees part of her poking out. He fires.

She's hit. Shoulder.

She twists back behind the car. "Oh, God, he shot me!" She drops the gun and flops over. "The jerk."

Philip says, "Bloody hell."

Norman picks up the gun. He's done with this joker. "This is over, right now it is," he says.

Casey says, "There may not be any bullets."

"Then I'll throw it."

Jerry keeps veering to the left to come around the hood to get a clear view and open fire. He stops. Did he hear a growl? A snarl? From the woods?

Bushes move and Vicious is charging at him.

"Damn beast from hell!"

He raises his gun but too late to shoot as Vicious leaps at his throat and – Smack! – Jerry wacks her with the butt of the gun and sends her sprawling.

The Pekingese rolls over and lays still.

Norman is up from behind the car, aims at Jerry and pulls the trigger. *Click. Click. Click.* "Shit!"

Jerry scowls at him, slowly raises his gun and aims, he locks Norman's chest in his sight line. Norman closes his eyes. A shot rings out.

Jerry falls to the ground.

Benjie stands on the edge of the wooded area. He lowers his gun.

Earl is up and moving, getting close, his gun raised he stops in front of Benjie. He looks over to the fallen Jerry Broom and back to his son.

"You were supposed to be a team player," Earl says.

"I am a team player, Dad. It's just that we're not on the same team anymore."

There is a silence. Jerry lays on the ground. Reverend Broom is standing behind the Mercury. Philip and the wounded Casey are up from behind the Honda. Norman stands ahead in of them. And Earl Porter's gun continues to point directly at his son.

Here's this: Earl has had enough. The Reverend doesn't matter, jail doesn't matter, not even the rapture matters. *It's his son*. He drops the gun.

Norman walks over and picks it up.

Reverend Broom is out from behind the Mercury. Jerry? Shot? Is he dead? He is by his fallen boy and kneeling, resting his head in his lap. Blood trickles from Jerry's mouth and there's a deep wound in his chest.

"Oh my poor obedient boy."

In the distance a siren is heard. Harvey on the way.

Philip goes to Vicious and picks her up. Her eyes are open, she whimpers and licks his face. "There's a good girl," Philip says.

Norman and Casey examine her wound. There's little bleeding, the bullet went right through and she will be okay. But she can't drive.

Benjie Porter is at the stolen car and finds the keys are in the ignition. He watched his father setting up the wires and believes he has a chance to disarm the explosive device. It is time to keep his promises.

"We can take the Mercury," he tells Norman. "It'll be faster and we don't have much time."

Benjie jumps in as Norman runs to join him.

37.

As Norman hurtles in the Mercury toward his family's transplanted motor home, his parents are three miles to the northeast. James and Lana are breaking up camp atop Mt. Bowen, a 1,025 meter (3,357 feet) mountain next to Lake Still Waters. They're returning home.

Or so they think.

"You didn't do much worrying up here," James tells his wife. "Mountain air must have been agreeable. Or it was the swim courtesy my brother. Got the worrying out of your system."

"So I don't worry too much, after all?" she replies, picking up two tin cups and stuffing them into a pack with more force than necessary. "How generous of you."

"Same for me," he hastily adds, sensing she's unhappy with being characterized as a worrier, again. "I cut down on my worry, too."

"Maybe there was nothing to worry about in the first place," Lana says. "Maybe our children are fine and the past is truly gone, forever."

"That is a nice thought. I will embrace it."

"So will I."

James says, "Speaking of embracing, we never did try that patch of grass overtop that ridge. Remember the one we found that first morning? With the view of the lake? Whaddaya say? One more for the road?"

There was a mischievous glint in James' eyes and Lana thought if he could have a mischievous glint in his eyes, she could have a mischievous glint in hers.

"Yes please," she said, with an exceedingly mischievous glint. "That would suit me nicely."

While Norman and Benjie were pulling up to the motor home, James and Lana were walking hand in hand atop a small mountain, walking toward a patch of grass that had a wonderful view of Lake Still Waters.

For the purpose of making love.

38.

Before Benjie has brought the car to a full stop Norman is out and running to the front door. He's so focused on Keeley and Riley that seeing his home surrounded by woods instead of in their yard barely registers.

"Don't touch anything," Benjie warns. "You could set it off."

On the ground by the front door there's a grey box with wires going up to the door handle before branching off in either direction and then going all the way around the home. There's a small screen in the box with a display that reads 2:41.

Norman grabs for the door handle.

"No!" Benjie is behind him. "Open it and you trip the wire."

"Keeley?! Riley?!" Muffled sounds.

His brother and sister are locked in Keeley's room, bound and gagged in chairs. They were side-by-side but Riley now squirms on the floor, he tipped over while trying to loosen his ropes. He hears his brother's voice and renews his efforts to get free.

Keeley yells, "Norman, you promised!" With a gag over her mouth Norman can't be sure what he's hearing but they're in there and alive.

Benjie figures that opening any window or the door will produce the same result - Boom! He looks at the grey box. Five wires. So which does what?

"What wire do we cut first?" Norman asks.

"He said three are just there to confuse and nothing happens if they're cut. There's one, if it's cut it will disarm the bomb and one that sends a charge to the explosives under your propane tanks."

"And blows the place up."

"I'm afraid so."

Benjie pulls out the Swiss Army knife he took from Riley in the driveway of the Broom mansion.

"You'll be safer by the trees."

"I'm not going anywhere." Norman looks to the counter: 2:13. "I don't like these odds," he says. "There has to be another way."

"If you think of one, let me know. But make it fast."

Inside, tied into the chair, Riley crawls to the door and kicks at it, trying to let Norman know where they are. Keeley is yelling.

Norman says, "Hear that? Start cutting."

Benjie puts the knife to a wire. "He put the three fakes in first, in the middle, and the real ones on either side. So would you agree these three are in the middle."

"These ones, yes" Norman touches them. "Go ahead."

Benjie snips one of the ones in the middle. Nothing. Puts the knife up against another. Snips. They're still there. Benjie looks at Norman. Norman nods. Benjie snips the third middle wire. No explosion.

But the timer still moves.

Of the two left, one disarms, one ignites. Moving his knife under one of the remaining wires, poised to cut, he looks up to Norman.

"Fifty-fifty chance," Benjie says. "Your call."

As Norman looks at the timer again his gaze crosses the door's tiny window. There's no wire attached to it.

"I have a better idea," Norman says. "The door's window. I can slip through there."

"That's not much of an opening."

"I did it once before when I locked myself out."

"Okay. Only how long ago was that?"

"I was 14, but I can still do it."

"You been on a bus before, right? Like a Greyhound?"

"Of course I been on a bus."

"That's about the same size as a bus window."

"I can get through it."

Norman has a rock and shatters the glass. There are shards left on the top frame; Benjie reaches up to break them off but Norman can't wait, he grabs the ledge, pulls up and his head is in. Benjie shoves his lower legs up and now Norman's shoulders are through. It's tight and a glass shard is cutting along Norman's back as he inches forward.

"Aaahhhh!"

Benjie stops pushing. Partially inside, his voice muffled, Norman yells, "Keep going!"

Norman's foot nearly kicks a wire on the door handle but Benjie lifts it and cups a hand under each foot and pushes up and forward. Norman squeezes through to his ass and with more of him inside than out the weight of his upper body pulls him down and his legs disappear from Benjie's view. Thump! He falls to the floor. Norman is inside.

Benjie checks the time: 1:28

Rushing to Keeley's door, Norman bends down to the slot: "I'm here, hang in there, I'm coming." Muffled reactions from inside the room.

Examining the door, Norman finds three deadbolts have been attached. How is he gonna break three deadbolts in seconds? He remembers what Riley gave Keeley at breakfast to cut her muffin with the day the motor home was stolen and throws open the storage cupboard and grabs the fire ax.

The first two swings hit the mark and each breaks a lock. One more. The third swing does not break the third lock. Swings again, doesn't break it.

Outside, Benjie has cleared all the glass shards from the window. He looks to the display on the timer. "Fifty-eight seconds!" he shouts.

Norman takes three steps back and rushes up to the door and swings the ax. The lock snaps off and he kicks the door open.

He's in.

No other way but to rip the duct tape off Keeley's mouth. She doesn't care about pain, she's focused on something else and when her mouth is free she lets him know it.

"What about your promise?" she demands. "You said you were never, ever, ever going to leave me BUT YOU DID!"

"Could we talk about this later?" he asks, untying her.

"Okay, but I'm still mad at you."

He has her free and quickly turns to Riley, pulls his chair back up to standing and rips off his duct tape and starts untying his hands.

"No," Riley yells. "Get her out first."

Norman gives his brother the thumbs up, tousles his hair, grabs

Keeley and heads to the front door.

"It's wired," he tells her. "Climb through the window."

Keeley says, "But what about Riley?"

"Don't worry, I'll get him." She puts her foot in his hand and he lifts her.

Benjie calls out, "What's going on in there?"

"Keeley's coming out!" Norman turns to her. "Mister-Nice guy is there. You can trust him."

He cups his hands and up she goes and she's through. On the other side, Benjie grabs her shoulders and pulls her down and stands her up.

"Run," he tells her. "Behind the car."

Hands untied, Riley unbinds one foot, Norman the other. Riley's free and out they go. Teenage boys are made for this kind of thing and Riley is through the window in seconds. He falls out on the other side.

Norman pulls himself up and gets his head and shoulder out the window. Without shards of glass to impede him this time it's easier and Benjie and Riley grab him, yank and – they all fall in a heap. Norman is out.

"Let's go," Benjie shouts.

Benjie and Norman sprint to the car. Keeley throws her arms around her big brother and hugs. "Thank you for not leaving me," she says.

Benjie points back to the motor home, "Hey, your brother. Look." Riley is still back there, examining the wires and about to cut one.

"Riley, no!" Norman rushes to him.

"I know what you do," Riley says. "You just cut them."

Norman grabs his arm. "You could cut the wrong one! Come on. We don't need it anymore!" Timer says: four seconds. They run for the car and dive behind it.

Boom!

Debris flies up toward the sky. The motor home has been raptured.

After the pieces have landed, the four stand and look at what is left. While some of the outer wall remains most of the roof is gone and the interior all but gutted. There's a fire where the front door once stood, another burns in the room Keeley was held captive in. There's a small fire in the woods where debris landed.

They find a blanket in the trunk of the car and use it to smother fires. Norman sees there's virtually nothing from the interior worth saving. Given what might have been he doesn't really care.

Harvey and another officer arrive. Harvey tells them he arrested Reverend Broom and Earl Porter and that Jerry may not make it. Quietly, Benjie mouths a silent prayer before being arrested for his role in the kidnapping. As Harvey puts cuffs on him, Riley watches.

"Hey Benjie," Riley says. "Thanks for being one of those people who keep their promises."

Benjie smiles and nods, "You take care of your sister. Not that she needs it."

"Always."

Philip pulls up in the Honda. Paramedics took Casey to the hospital but not before she recorded a message for Norman on Philip's phone. Philip gives it to Norman, who moves off to listen in private.

Her messages says: *I know you'll get this message because I know you will save your family and you will survive. So congratulations for rescuing them and getting them back. If you want something done in this world – ask Norman Hapgood. He is a man of action.*

She believed in him.

He thinks how neither he nor his family would have made it without Casey. He listens to her message again. And again.

Agnes and Margaret arrive and start to film.

39.

While their sons and daughter were crouching behind a 70s era Ford Mercury as their motor home blew up, James and Lana Miller, soon to again be James and Lana Hapgood, were completing their embracing on the patch of grass with a view.

The two heard the explosion and found the timing of it appropriate, for it came just as they finished embracing, the both of them, together.

"That was nice timing," Lana purrs.

"It certainly was," James says, smiling contentedly. "Hydro must be clearing that land early."

"I prefer to think of it as the Gods arranging a spectacular finish to our vacation."

"I hope Norman got the story."

"Oh, I'm sure he's right where the action is."

The two return to their camp and finish gathering up gear and garbage and are soon hoisting packsacks.

Hand in hand, James and Lana begin the hike home, the first trip they've taken without their children now successfully completed.

40.

It's a bright summer evening in the town of Still Waters, British Columbia, the temperature having climbed since a summer squall a week before. We are in a typical, small town neighbourhood, but one yard stands out. In the Hapgood yard something has been added. Now, along with a shed, a badminton net, a hockey net and hockey sticks, there is a sign that announces the family's intentions for their property.

We shall get to that sign.

Across the street is the home of Agnes and Margaret; a dog named Vicious is on the porch, barking to be let inside. The door opens and in she goes. Voices waft into the night air before the door is closed.

In Agnes and Margaret's living-room people gather around a TV, some are standing, others sit on a couch, in chairs or on the floor. They are having a grand time watching a movie each of them plays a role in.

James and Lana are there. The two were in for surprises upon their return from a camping trip and heard fantastical stories they could scarcely believe.

Agnes and Margaret are on the couch with Casey, her wounded shoulder in a sling. Riley and Keeley are on the floor and in a chair is Cpl. Harvey Kwong.

Standing in a corner is Jack Hapgood; committed to sobriety once again, he has more desire to succeed than ever. On the other side of the room stands Philip Briggs, who likewise has given up the bottle; Philip is munching on his third piece of bannock.

Vicious is cuddling at his legs.

Norman enters from the kitchen. "I put another kettle on for more tea."

Lana says, "Who's got the remote? Let's watch it again!"

"I got it," Riley calls out, hitting play.

"It's the best movie ever!" Keeley says yells as Norman settles in next to her.

The TV screen lights up and coming into focus is Agnes and Margaret's film. There is plenty of action and it serves as a recapping of the adventures the Hapgood family, once known as the Miller family, have recently been through.

The crowd cheers at the start as they watch Norman trying to cross a street. The footage from the night the motor home went missing, with Harvey arriving and Norman lamenting, is brief, for Agnes and Margaret did not want to intrude upon a scene of grief. There's Casey and Riley bringing Norman coffee and donuts in the empty yard, filmed from Agnes and Margaret's upper story window. Jack arrives with Norman's bank card.

Riley gets on the bus and there are cheers when the hesitant Norman climbs aboard. Shots of the brothers and Casey coming out of the bus depot in Vancouver and walking past Casey's apartment. Philip is seen spilling his golf clubs on the sidewalk.

"Bloody embarrassing," Philip mutters aloud.

There's Norman negotiating a revolving door at the motor vehicle branch. Casey expertly crosses a busy Vancouver street to talk to the filmmakers. Riley hangs out the Honda's window, yelling "Hi Mom, hi Dad. Having a wonderful time only Norman is a wimp!"

James says, "Thanks for thinking of us, Riley."

"Hey, hold on," Norman says. "What about a lecture for name-calling?"

"You deserved it," Riley says. "Then. Not now."

Keeley says, "Now he's my hero." She leans over to kiss Norman's cheek.

James and Lana love seeing the adventures they missed, just watching their oldest son get on a bus and walk down the streets of the city is a thrill. Norman in Vancouver!

"Fabulous," his mother shouts "Norman, you and I are going for a weekend in the city."

The film has car chases and even Jerry and Benjie are there, briefly seen in the Cadillac as they nearly sideswipe Agnes and Margaret in their rental.

Riley asks Harvey what Benjie's chances of avoiding jail are and he tells him there is no chance.

"But he won't be charged in the death of Jerry Broom," Harvey adds. "And the Crown Attorney is lowering his charge from kidnapping to accessory after the fact. Earl Porter is testifying his son didn't enter the mobile home until after it was driven off the lot and was unaware Keeley was inside it."

The fathers, Harvey tells everyone, may spend the rest of their lives behind bars.

The film continues. There's Norman crossing a road, this time with confidence, on his way to tell Casey about what a 'ga' is. Philip drives up and Norman stalls the car. A loud cheer when Casey gets behind the wheel.

Agnes and Margaret had followed Harvey to the scene of the stand-off and there's footage of the arrests of Reverend Broom and Earl Porter. That gets applause.

Harvey gave them a copy of the footage from the camera mounted in a tree across from the motor home and they watch Benjie cut wires and Norman squeeze through the window. It falls quiet as Keeley and Riley and finally Norman tumble out the window.

Lana elicits an "Oh God" when Riley picks up the detonator and looks as if he is going to cut a wire. "You are so lucky to have your big brother," she says.

Norman and Riley run out of frame. There is a collective gasp when the home blows up. It's incredible to see and there is silence as they watch the debris that was once the Miller family home float down to earth.

There are shots of a visit to Casey in the hospital and of James and Lana arriving home and finding they no longer have a home. Agnes and Margaret filmed the two walking up to the yard, capturing shock on their faces upon seeing it empty.

The film ends with Norman in the yard and hammering that sign into the ground; it says: *Coming soon to this space: New home THAT DOES NOT MOVE.*

That scene gets the biggest cheer of all.

"Wow." James says. "You know I gotta say it: you two did an extraordinary job of keeping an eye on our kids. Thank you so much."

Lana adds, "Obviously no reason to worry about what the kids are up to while we're away." That gets a laugh.

"I would like to say something to Agnes and Margaret." Jack suddenly says. "You are damn fine reporters and I can't tell you how much it means to see the arrest of the men who took Patty and Mac from me. I never thought I'd see it and I am forever grateful. Thank you."

Agnes and Margaret stand up.

"You are welcome," Margaret says. "We feel privileged to have played a small role in bringing light into a dark matter. Making this film was not for the faint of heart but it was an experience we will cherish always."

"It is a gift from our hearts," Agnes adds, looking to James and Lana. "You accepted us at a time when that was too rare. Consider this payback for the joy of being your neighbours all of these wonderful years. We love you all."

Applause. Lana wipes a tear. So does James. They get up and go to their neighbours and hugs are shared. It takes a few moments. More applause.

Keeley grabs the remote, "Rewind!"

Philip asks how the tea is coming along and Casey asks Riley if the British and their penchant for tea isn't a cliché. He says maybe but he's letting clichés go now.

"I don't want to ritualize my response to them," he says. Norman asks where he learnt the word 'ritualize' and Riley says he must have read it.

"Good, keep reading," Norman tells him. "And Philip, I'll be happy to get you another tea. Anybody else?" Norman counts hands.

Casey follows him into the kitchen. It's the first time they've been alone since the rescue. Standing next to one another, they lean against the counter.

Norman says, "Hard to believe it all really happened."

"It's still sinking in. How is your Uncle Jack doing?"

"Seems to like us. Keeley is thrilled to have an uncle and my dad is happy to have a brother again. They had a long talk about Patty and Mac. We're all going to Vancouver to put flowers on their grave. You're invited."

"Of course I'll come."

"How is your shoulder?" he moves away a bit. "I don't wanna bump it."

She slides back toward him. "It's fine. Cast off in a week. I accepted my parent's plane ticket, by the way. Visiting them in Truro, Nova Scotia."

"That's great."

"Yeah. Just for a week. I might get bored any longer."

"That's a start."

"What about you? How're you doing?"

"Good. Everything makes sense now." Pause. He looks at her. "You know you are a great detective. You're smart and brave and my family wouldn't be here if you hadn't bugged that telephone booth."

"Thanks but The Case of The Miller-Hapgood Family was my first, and last. I am officially out of the detective business. Not that I was ever officially in."

"Really? Why?"

"For one, turns out I don't enjoy being shot. Who'd 'a thunk that, hey?"

Norman smiles. He wants to say something; he hesitates a moment then plunges on. "Say, did my parents tell you they're building the new house themselves? A modern two-story. They'll get help from a local contractor but it's mostly gonna be them."

"Sweet."

"Jack will be part of the crew and I am being left to run the Current on my own. With Riley and Keeley."

"Two veteran reporters."

"Yes and no. They only write about things they like and then only if they feel like it, which isn't often. I'll have to sell ads, do the interviews, write stories, take the photos, do the layout."

"That's a lot to take on."

"Yeah. You ever worked on a newspaper?"

"I did. I wrote a story, once. It was about a pumpkin."

"I remember that. It was very well written."

"I seem to recall problems with my lead."

"Nope. It was colorful with nice alliteration." He moves closer. "Here's this: I was thinking that when you get back you might consider joining the Current staff." He is very close to her now. "Beats getting shot at."

"Come to think of it, being connected to you would beat getting shot at." She leans in and they kiss, deep and long.

Up for air.

Norman says, "It's a long haul, learning the business. I expect you'd catch on easily enough but you'd have to commit."

"I don't think that would be a problem," she says. "Not this time it won't."

They kiss again.

In the living-room another showing of the film ends and there is a round of applause and a big, big cheer.

41.

Casey was not in the least bored during her trip to Nova Scotia. She went hiking, tidal bore rafting on the Shubenacadie River, she even visited the historic lighthouse at Peggy's Cove. They ate lobster nightly.

Her parents told Casey how much they loved her and she told them she loved them. They explained their job opportunities came suddenly and that they had been needed right away. Their hope was that she would stay in Nova Scoita, perhaps study at Dalhousie, under an hour away from their home.

She told them she'd be learning as she worked in her new job on a community newspaper in the town of Still Waters. They were happy for her and she returned to B.C. feeling a great warmth for her family.

Casey quickly fell in love with working on a newspaper. She enjoyed interviewing people, pitching ad ideas to business owners, taking photos, she even enjoyed doing layout, which she came to excell at.

Her writing improved so quickly that after a month Norman sent her to cover her first council meeting. She came back with a story about a new by-law making it illegal to hit golf balls into Bluewater Park (which, apparently, had recently been done).

Her headline? *Brazen by-law bans bashing of balls into Bluewater*. Norman liked the alliteration well enough but chopped 'brazen' from the top and put it in front of 'bashing.' The by-law wasn't brazen, he explained, but bashing balls into Bluewater was.

Two months after Casey and Norman started working together they began living together in an apartment with a room for Riley. The walk to work requires crossing two intersections, which Norman easily manages.

For now Keeley and her parents still live in back of the newspaper offices. Each weekday morning Keeley's over-protective brother Riley arrives to walk with her to school. They often stop and get her peach juice and a raspberry muffin at Alf's Cafe.

James and Lana leave the office each weekday morning to work with Jack on building the family's new home.

Philip moved to Still Waters and started his own IT business. He and Jack go to AA meetings together. He plays in the co-ed soccer league and lives with Ann; they met when she teased him about his having called her a "stalwart defender" in a soccer story he wrote for the paper. The two are often seen taking their dog Vicious for walks in Bluewater Park.

And finally, Casey and Norman took on a book project, collecting together each of their notes to write about the family's adventures.

Within that story we, yes *we*, for it was the two of us who wrote the story you are reading, included the bugging of the phone booth and all the events the family became caught up in.

We conducted many interviews, from prison even Earl and Broom were helpful. Benjie was a great source of information and promised to vist upon his release.

In the best new journalism tradition we put you the reader in the midst of the action by the use of direct quotes. Reporters rarely write in the first person so until this final chapter we employed a third person, omniscient narrator.

To avoid the spotlight we used a pseudonym, a literary tradition employed by authors such as Jane Austen and Steven King.

So it is that we published *Leaving Still Waters* under the name 'Marcus Cary Hondro.'

Thanks for reading our story.

Oh, one more thing: If you want something done in this world you must be prepared to do it yourself. If you want it badly enough you will manage it.

(Cliché be damned.)

Casey Collier and Norman Hapgood
July 3, 2018

Manufactured by Amazon.ca
Bolton, ON

10508904R00152